應用外語
28

餐旅英語
{ 會話 }

潘朝達・編著

五南圖書出版公司 印行

ENGLISH

-前言-

現代科技的突飛猛進,提供了更為快捷的運輸與資訊,令人感覺到,地球越來越小,距離也越來越近了。在國際一片和平自由的氣氛中,過去視為旅遊的禁區,現在幾乎已經全部解除了。

國人可以自由自在的到世界各地觀光旅遊,洽談商務,參加會議或研究開發。而台灣也成為世界主要經貿中心之一,國際人士來往頻繁,加深了英語的強烈需求。

英語是國際語言,會說英語,易與人直接溝通,增進瞭解;通曉英語,更能立即而確實的,獲得國際重要的第一手資訊,搶得先機。要做現代人,不能不多學習英語。

住宿與飲食,是人類的基本需求,然而,在溫飽之餘,國人應共同建立正確而富有的住宿與飲食文化。

本書針對住宿與飲食方面,提供專業英語會話,以及專業常識做為參考,但願能有助益。由於編印過程中,難免疏忽,希望讀者給予批評指教。

潘朝達—於臺北市

- 目次 -

Chapter 2 RESTAURANT 餐廳

Chapter 1 HOTEL飯店、旅館

- 一、接待業務
- 二、從業人員

一 接待業務

Receptionist
Good evening, sir. What may I do for you tonight?
晚安，先生。什麼事情要我幫忙的嗎？

Dr. Mc.
I'm Dr. Edward L. Mcintosh from San Francisco, California. I've come for the annual surgery medical convention. A room has been reserved for me, hasn't it?
我是愛得華麥堅圖醫生，從加州舊金山來的。我來這裡參加外科醫學年會，我訂的房間是否已經保留給我了！

Receptionist
Dr. Edward Mcintosh. Let me see. No, Doctor. Your name is not on the list. When did you make your reservation? Did you make it yourself?
麥堅圖醫生。我看一下。沒有耶，醫生。訂房單上沒有您的名字，您什麼時候訂的？是您自己訂的嗎？

Dr. Mc.
No, I didn't make the reservation myself. Mr. Foreman, who was coming here from Los Angeles, promised to reserve a room for me.
不，不是我自己訂的。是福門先生代訂的，他從洛杉磯來這裡，答應幫我訂下房間的。

Receptionist
Did you receive confirmation from us, Doctor?
您收到我們的訂房確認嗎？醫生。

Dr. Mc.
No, I didn't. But Mr. Foreman gave you a deposit, didn't he?
沒有。但福門先生付了訂金的，他沒付嗎？

Receptionist
I'm sorry, but he didn't. There must be some mistake.
對不起，他沒付訂金。一定有些錯誤。

002

Dr. Mc. I know it's late, but may I speak to Mr. Foreman?
我知道很晚了，但我可以和福門先生說話嗎？

Receptionist I'm sorry, Doctor, but the Foremans left this morning.
對不起，醫生，福門一家人已經在今天早上，離開這裡了。

Dr. Mc. Oh no! Of course, I can blame only myself. I should attend to my own business myself. Surely you have a single room vacant, haven't you?
哦！糟了！當然，我只怪自己，這些事應該自己來做。你應該還有一間空的單人房吧？

Receptionist I'm sorry, Dr. Mcintosh. There is full occupancy tonight. However, we will find accommodation for you in another hotel. (To his assistant) Peter, call the Carlton Hotel and tell them that we need a room for Dr. Mcintosh.
對不起，麥醫生。今晚客滿了。不過，我們會替您找到房間住的。（面對他的助手）彼得，打電話到嘉登大飯店，告訴他們說，我們要個房間給麥醫生。

Dr. Mc. A message was left for me, wasn't it?A letter from Dr. Kent?
有沒有字條留給我的？有肯特醫生給我的信嗎？

Receptionist (After looking through the reserved mail)
No, Doctor. I can't find anything here for you.
You are having bad luck tonight.
（看過預留信件後）沒有，醫生。沒有任何東西是要留給您的。今晚您的運氣真不好。

Peter (Returning) The Carlton Hotel will take Dr. Mcintosh.
（走回來）嘉登大飯店有房間給麥醫生。

Receptionist That's better luck. Dr. Mcintosh, we'll send you to the Carlton Hotel by taxi, and we'll also pay for your hotel room tonight. I'm sure that we'll have a checkout in the morning. I'll call you as soon as we know. Have a good night's sleep.

運氣還不錯。麥醫生,我們叫計程車送您到嘉登大飯店,今晚的房租我們付。明早有人遷出時,我會儘快通知您(意即搬回來),祝您有個好夢。

Dr. Mc. Thank you. I appreciate what you are doing for me. You won't forget me, will you? I want to stay here because our meetings are held here.

謝謝。我很感激你替我所做的安排。可別忘了我,我要住在這裡,因為我們的會議在這裡舉行。

Peter Your taxi is waiting, sir.

計程車在等您了,先生。

Dr. Mc. Thank you. Good night.

謝謝。晚安。

VOCABULARY & IDIOMS

- reservation 訂房。
- doctor (Dr.) 醫師；博士。
- Annual surgery Medical Convention 外科醫學年會。
- Convention 大會。
- promise 保證；答應。
- receive 接到。
- confirmation 認定、確定。
- deposit 預付訂金。
- mistake 錯誤。
- blame 責怪。
- own business 自己的事。
- vacant 空（房）。
- full occupancy 客滿。
- accommodation 合適住的地方。
- reserved mail 保留的函件。
- bad luck 壞運氣。
- better luck 還好。
- appreciate 感謝。
- held here 在這裡舉行。

1. 電話傳真訂房函 Fax reservation

8450737 Marriott Hotel, H.K.
4/10.90

TO: RESERVATION MANAGER, MARRIOTT HOTEL, HK
FROM: PETER C.T. PAN, TAIPEI, TAIWAN

PLEASE RESERVE A SINGLE ROOM WITH BATH FROM THE
EVENING OF MAY 20th TO 26th 2017. A. QUIET ROOM ON A
LOWER FLOOR AWAY FROM THE STREET IS PREFERRED.
PLEASE CONFIRM AS SOON AS POSSIBLE AND INFORM ME
IF A DEPOSIT IS REQUIRED.

PETER C.T. PAN
FAX NUMBER: (02)777-2222 TAIPET,
E-MAIL: 1234@gmail.com

reservation manager 訂房經理。

a single room with bath 一間有浴廁的單人房。

quiet room 安靜的房間。

lower floor 低樓層。

confirm 確認。

deposit 訂金。

required 要求的。

❷ 旅館房租的標示

Single Occupancy　住一人
Double Occupancy　住二人
Executive Suites　商務套房
Deluxe Suites　豪華套房
Additional Person　加住一人
Checkout time: Noon
每天中午12點結帳，如果不
續住，中午12點以前要結帳
退房，逾時未結帳，則加收
房租。

SCHEDULE OF GUEST ROOM RATES

Single Occupancy

$110.00

$120.00

$130.00

Double Occupancy

$125.00

$135.00

$145.00

Executive Suites

$150-$165

Deluxe Suites

$350-$1000

Additional Person-$15.00

Accomodations subject to 7% room tax

Cbeckout time: Noon

Rates subject to change without notice

326 BROADWAY, SAN DIEGO, CALIFORNIA 92101

FOR INFORMATION OR RESERVATIONS, CALL

(619) 232-3121.

IN CALIFORNIA, CALL TOLL FREE 1-800-542-6082.

IN LOS ANGELES, CALL 1-213-759-1800.

IN CONTINENTAL U.S. CALL 1-800-854-2608.

IN CANADA CALL 1-800-854-6742. TELEX: 183-881.

2. Check-in 入住 🔊 1-1-2

Receptionist
(Smiling) Good morning, sir. May I help you?
（微笑著）先生，早安，我能為您效勞嗎？

Mr. Foreman
Yes, I'm Billy Foreman. Do you have a reservation for me and my family?
好的，我叫比利‧福門，請查一下我們的訂房好嗎？

Receptionist
Mr. Billy Foreman...Wait a minute, please. I'll check the list. (Receptionist check the list)Yes, we have your reservation. Mr. and Mrs. Foreman, two boys and one girl. Two double rooms and one single. One double room has a double bed and has twin beds. The single room has a single bed.
福門先生……請等一下，讓我看一下名單（查訂房單）是的，有您的訂房，福門先生和太太、二位男孩、一位女孩。要二間雙人房、一間單人房，雙人房一間要一張雙人床，另一間要二張單人床，單人房要單人床。

Mr. Foreman
That's right.
對了。

Receptionist
Very good, sir. Will you please register? Kindly sign your name on this card.
好極了，先生，請您登記好嗎？麻煩您在這張登記卡簽上您的名字。

Mr. Foreman
What are the rates for the rooms?
房間的價錢多少？

Receptionist
The rates are right here on this card, sir. Double rooms are three thousand NT dollars per day. A single room is two thousand five hundred dollars.

房價在這卡片上有寫，先生，雙人房是一天3,000元，單人房是2,500元。

Mr. Foreman
Is there a special rate by the week?
住一星期有沒有特別優惠呢？（意思是有沒有折扣）

Receptionist
Yes, there is a ten percent discount.
有的，可以打九折。

Mr. Foreman
That's fine.
那很好。

Receptionist
May I look at your passports for a moment, sir?
先生，您們的護照都讓我看一下好嗎？

Mr. Foreman
Yes, here they are.
可以的，都在這兒。

Receptionist
Thank you, sir. I'll send them up right away.
謝謝您，先生，我會立即送回給您的。

front desk 飯店的接待櫃檯

VOCABULARY & IDIOMS

- check-in 旅客到達旅館，辦理登記手續「住進旅館」之意。
- front desk 大廳櫃檯，辦理旅客登記手續。
- Receptionist 接待員。
- smiling 微笑著。
- May I help you? 客氣語，直譯爲「我能幫你忙嗎？」。
- reservation 預約、預訂旅館客房或餐廳座位、飛機座位等。
- family 家庭、家族。
- just a minute 等一會兒。
- list 單。name list名單。
- double room 雙人房。
- single 單一的、單獨的，亦作單身解。
- double bed 雙人床。
- twin bed 兩張床。
- single bed 單人床。
- register 登記。
- sign 簽名、簽字；記號、符號。
- name 名字（姓爲Surname or Last name，名爲First name）。
- card 卡。信用卡credit card。
- rate 租金。
- NT$ 新台幣New Taiwan dollar的簡寫。
- per day 一天，按日。
- special rate 特別租金。
- discount 折扣、優待。
- look at 看看。

- passport　護照。
- Thank you, sir.　謝謝您，先生（禮貌用語）。
- right away　立刻、馬上。
- check　核對使之正確。
- sir　先生、閣下（表示有禮、敬意）。
- mister　先生。簡寫Mr.注意句點。
- madam　夫人、女士（對婦女的尊敬稱呼）。
- Mrs.　夫人、太太。注意句點（已婚婦女）。
- Miss　未婚小姐。注意不可加句點。

　　　　小寫miss是懷念、失誤之意。
- lady　淑女、貴婦。男士則稱gentleman。

Mr. Foreman　Are the rooms next to each other?
房間是不是連在一起的？

Receptionist　Unfortunately, no. Two are next to each other and one is across the hall.
很抱歉，不是的。二間連在一起，另一間要穿越走廊。

Mr. Foreman　That's too bad. I prefer adjoining rooms.
真糟糕！我喜歡連在一起的房間。

Receptionist　I'm sorry, sir. We can't give you three rooms together today. How about a suite?
對不起，先生。今天沒有三間房間連在一起的，套房好嗎？

Mr. Foreman　How many rooms are in a suite?
套房裡有幾個房間？

Receptionist　We have a very nice suite with two bedrooms and a living room. The living room has a convertible sofa.
我們有一間很好的套房，裡面有二間臥室，一間客廳。客廳有一張沙發床。

Mr. Foreman　How much does it cost?
房租多少？

Receptionist　The daily rate for this one is six thousand dollars, and the weekly rate is thirty-three thousand six hundred.
一天是6,000元，一星期算33,600元。

Mr. Foreman　Which floor is it on?
在那層樓？

Receptionist

It's on the fifth floor, facing the park. It has a lovely view.

在五樓，面向著公園，視野很好。

Mr. Foreman

O.K. Give us the suite for a week. (To Mrs. Foreman) What do you think about that, dear? (He signs the registration card.)

好吧，給我們這間套房，住一星期。（轉向福門太太）親愛的，妳的意見如何？（他在登記簽字。）

Mrs. Foreman

That's fine, Billy. I'd like that.

很好，比利，我很喜歡。

Receptionist

Very well sir. It's suite 1502. I'm sure you will find everything satisfactory. If you need anything, please call us. I hope you enjoy your stay in our hotel. Bellman, here are the key to 1502. Take the guests up to their rooms, please.

很好，先生。這是1502號套房，我相信您會覺得滿意的，如果有什麼要吩咐，請告訴我們，我希望您住在這裡會感到十分的愉快。行李員，這是1502房的鑰匙，請帶客人上去他們的房間。

Bellman

Yes, sir. This way, please. (Picking up a briefcase.) Isn't this your briefcase, sir?

是的，先生。請走這邊。（提起一件公事包）這是您的公事包嗎？先生。

Mr. Foreman

Indeed it is. Thanks.

沒錯，謝謝。

Danny

Where is my little blue bag?

我的藍色小袋子呢？

Allen

Oh, Danny. The bellman brings the luggage on his cart.

哦！丹尼，行李員把它放在行李車上了。

Danny Whose bags are those? (He walks toward the door.)
這是誰的行李？（他往大門走去。）

Mrs. Foreman Danny don't go away. Come, children. Get in the elevator. The elevator operator is waiting.
丹尼不要走開，孩子們快來進電梯！電梯服務員在等我們了。

- next to each other　互相緊鄰。
- unfortunately　不幸、不巧。
- across the hall　越過走廊。
- adjoining room　相鄰房。
- I'm sorry, sir.　對不起，先生（禮貌用語）。
- suite　套房。
- bedroom　臥房（室）。
- living room　客廳。
- convertible sofa　沙發床。
- cost　成本、價值、價錢。
- daily rate　日租。
- weekly rate　週租。
- monthly rate　月租。
- on season rate　旺季（亦稱high season）租金。
- off season rate　淡季（亦稱low season）租金。
- floor　樓層。
- facing park　面向公園。
- lovely　可愛的、美好的。
- view　風景、景觀。
- O. K.　沒有問題。
- dear　親愛的（口頭語）。
- registration card　登記卡。
- Very well, sir　很好，先生（客氣用語）。
- satisfactory　滿意。

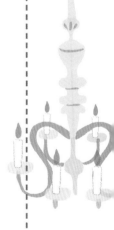

- hope　希望。
- key/room key　鑰匙／房間鑰匙。
- Yes, sir.　是的，先生（客氣用語）。
- This way, please.　請走這邊（客氣用語）。
- picking up　提起來、拿起來。
- briefcase　公事包、小型手提箱。
- bag　袋子。
- luggage/baggage　行李（較大件的）。
- cart　載運行李的推車。
- elevator　電梯。
- elevator operator　電梯操作員或服務員。
- porter/bellman　行李員。

1. 客房的種類及型式

1. 基本分類：

　(1) 單人房　無浴室　Single room without bath

　(2) 單人房　附淋浴　Single room with shower

　(3) 單人房　附浴室　Single room with bath (SWB)

　(4) 雙入房　無浴室　Double/Twin room without bath

　(5) 雙人房　附淋浴　Double/Twin room with shower

　(6) 雙人房　附浴室　Double/Twin room with bath (DWB/TWB)

2. 以床鋪分類：

    (1) 單人房　單人床　Single room with single bed

    (2) 單人房　雙人床　Single room with double bed

    (3) 單人房　沙發床　Single room with sofa bed

    (4) 雙人房　雙人床　Double room with double bed

    (5) 雙人房　2張單人床 Double room with 2 single bed

    (6) 雙人房　2張雙人床 Double room with 2 double bed

3. 以客房的位置分類

    (1) 向内房　Inside room　無窗或窗向天井的房間

    (2) 向外房　Outside room　窗向街道或景觀的房間

    (3) 連通房　Connecting room　房與房之間有門互相連通

    (4) 鄰接房　Adjoining room　緊鄰著的房間

4. 特別套房

    (1) 普通套房 Junior suite

    除了有雙人房間，雙人床設備外，另有客廳及浴廁。

    (2) 高級套房 Executive suite（商務套房）

    大房間備具特大床鋪，客廳、雙套浴廁外，另有商務設施。

    (3) 豪華套房 Deluxe suite

    大房間特大床鋪，客廳、高級家俱、地毯。影視音響，2套以上設備豪華的浴廁。

關於套房的認知歐美人和國人略有差異：
歐美人稱套房（suite）是指臥室除有全套衛浴設備外，至少還要有會客室（living room）。而國人稱套房，則指有衛浴設備的房間就是套房。

❷ 床的尺寸（公分 / 寬×長）

單人床(Single/Twin)	100/120×200
雙人床（Double）	140/160×200
皇后床（Queen）	180×200
國王床（King）	200×200

twin bed (2 single bed combined)

單人床2張合併式

electronic locking system

現代電子客房門鎖

twin bed (2 double bed separated)

雙人床2張分開式

・說明：國際五星級飯店，大部份使用電腦卡片鎖，進住時設定密碼，退房時消除密碼，卡片無效。Message的傳遞也用電腦系統作業。

4. Information desk 詢問櫃檯 🔊 1-1-4

Receptionist
Good afternoon, sir. May I help you?
午安，先生。我能幫您的忙嗎？

Mr. Lin
Yes, please. I'm looking for a friend, Mr. Foreman. Can you tell me if he is in the hotel?
是的，我要找我的朋友福門先生，可不可以告訴我，他在旅館裡嗎？

Receptionist
Mr. Foreman? Wait a minute please. I'll see if he is registered. There are a lot of Foreman here today.
福門先生是嗎？請等一下，我看看他是否已經登記。今天有好幾位福門先生。

Mr. Lin
Mr. Billy Foreman from Los Angeles, California. Isn't he staying at this hotel? I recommended it to him.
他叫比利·福門，從加州洛杉磯來的，他不住這家旅館嗎？是我推薦他們來住的。

Receptionist
Yes, here's his name...Mr. and Mrs. Billy Foreman and family. They are in suite l502.
有了，這裡有他的名字……比利·福門夫婦和家人，他們住在1502號套房。

Mr. Lin
Will you please call his room? I'd like to talk to him.
請您幫我打個電話到他房間，我想和他講話。

Receptionist
You may call him on the house phone. It's over there behind the captain's desk.
請您用館內電話打給他，館內電話就在領班櫃檯的後面。

Mr. Lin

1502. Thanks. (Mr. Lin touches the number. He soon returns to the desk.) Excuse me, please, but no one answers in 1502.

1502號房，謝謝。（林先生按撥號碼，他很快又回到櫃檯。）對不起，1502號房沒有人在（沒人接電話）。

Receptionist

I'll see if his keys are in the boxes. Perhaps the Mr. Foreman's are in one of the other rooms of their suite, or at the swimming pool, or in the coffee shop. Can you wait a few minutes? I'll have the bellman page him.

我看看他的鑰匙在不在架子上，也許他們在套房的另外一間臥室或在游泳池或咖啡廳。請您稍等一下，我叫行李員找一找。

Mr. Lin

Thank you, but I can't wait. I have to go back to the office. I'm already late. May I leave a message, please?

謝謝你，但我不能等，我要趕回辦公室，已經遲到了。我可以留個字條嗎？

Receptionist

Of course. Here is a piece of paper and an envelope. (Mr. Lin writes a note.)

當然可以，這裡有紙和信封。（林先生正在寫留言。）

Mr. Lin

Will you kindly put this in Mr. Foreman's box?

麻煩你，把這字條放在他的留言箱裡好嗎？

Receptionist

Yes, indeed, sir, with pleasure.

是的，先生。這是我份內的事。

Mr. Lin

(Leaving) Thank you very much. Good-bye.

（將要離開）非常謝謝，再見。

Receptionist

You're welcome, sir. Good-bye.

不必客氣，先生。再見。

① 旅館房價的計算方式

1. European Plan (EP):　　　　　歐式計價—只計房價，不含餐費。

   (no meal)

2. American Plan (AP):　　　　　美式計價—房價包含三餐在內。

   Full Pension/board

   (3 meals)

3. Modified Ameriean Plan (MP): 修正美式計價—房價包含二餐在內。

   Half Pension/board

   (2 meals)

4. Continental Plan (CP)：　　　歐陸式計價—房價包含歐陸式早餐。

   (B & C)

5. Bermuda plan (BP)：　　　　百慕達計價—房價包含美式早餐。

   (B＋B)

□臺灣的國際觀光旅館採EP或BP計算方式□

- information desk　詢問櫃檯。
- looking for　找尋。
- a lot of　許多（數量上的）。
- Los Angeles　洛杉磯，美國加州的大都市。
- recommend　推薦、介紹。
- call　打電話。
- house phone　旅館裡的內線電話。
- captain's desk　行李領班服務台。
- touch　按（電話號碼）。
- number　號碼。telephone number電話號碼。
- Excuse me.　對不起（客氣用語）。
- no one　沒人。
- box(es)　箱子、盒子。
- their　他們的。
- swimming pool　游泳池。
- coffee shop　咖啡廳。
- page　叫人去找要找的人。page boy聽差的、小侍。
- message　口信、留言。
- envelope　信封、封套。
- with pleasure　樂意的、愉快的。
- You're welcome.　不用客氣（客氣用語）。

小小叮嚀

2. 數字／算術

1	（一）	one
10	（一拾）	ten
100	（一百）	one hundred
1,000	（一千）	one thousand
10,000	（一萬）	ten thousand
100,000	（十萬）	one hundred thousand
1,000,000	（百萬）	one million
10,000,000	（千萬）	ten million
100,000,000	（一億）	one hundred million

	美國	英國
10億	one billion	one thousand million
100億	ten billion	ten thousand million
1,000億	one hundred billion	one hundred thousand million
1兆	one trillion	one billion

加＋	plus, and
減－	minus, less
乘×	times
除÷	divided by
等於＝	equals, makes
分數3/4	three quarters
數目	10,206 ten thousand two hundred and six
	10,206 ten piont two ou six

Receptionist
(Pleasanty) Good afternoon, Mr. Foreman. How are you this afternoon?
（愉快的）午安，福門先生。下午玩得愉快嗎？

Mr. Foreman
Fine, thanks.
很好，謝謝。

Receptionist
Here's your key. The receptionist put this message in your box just now. (She hands Mr. Foreman the note.)
這是您的鑰匙，剛剛接待員才把這封留言放入您的留言箱。（她把字條給了福門先生。）

Mrs. Foreman
Who is it from, Billy?
是誰留的，比利？

Mr. Foreman
Listen, Rosanna. (He reads.) "Billy, welcome to our fair city. Will you and Rosanna come to dinner at our house this evening, Monday? Please call my office as soon as you can, 2788-2121. I'm in a hurry and can't wait to locate you...Paul Lin".
聽著，羅莎娜（他在讀）「比利，歡迎您來到我們這個優美的城市，您和夫人能否在星期一晚上，駕臨我家共進晚餐，請決定後立刻通知我，我辦公室的電話號碼是2788-2121，我很忙所以無法等您回來……保羅‧林」。

Mrs. Foreman
How nice! But look at my hair. I'll have to go to a beauty parlor. Is there a beauty parlor nearby?
真好，但看看我的頭髮，非到美容院去不可。這附近有沒有美容院？

Receptionist
There is a very good one in the hotel. It's on the mezzanine, on the left of the elevators, or you may go up the stairway and turn right.

我們旅館裡有一家很好的。在電梯左邊的夾層樓，也可以走樓梯，上去右轉就是了。

Mr. Foreman

I suppose that I'll have to go to the barber shop too. Where is it?
我想我也要到理髮廳去，在哪裡呢？

Receptionist

The barber shop is also on the mezzanine, across from the beauty parlor. Do you like sauna bath? There's one on the right of the barber shop.
理髮廳也在夾層樓，穿過美容院就到了。您喜歡蒸汽浴嗎？就在理髮廳的右邊。

Mr. Foreman

Say, that's an idea.
真是個好主意。

Mrs. Foreman

But our clothes! They need pressing.
我們的衣服需要燙一燙啊！

Receptionist

The valet will give you immediate service, Mrs. Foreman.
洗衣服務員會給您快燙的，福門太太。

Mrs. Foreman

I'll go up now and give the clothes to them.
我現在就上去把衣服交給他們。

Mrs. Foreman

Billy, what about the children? Doesn't Paul say anything about them? We can't leave them alone at night.
比利，孩子怎麼辦？保羅有沒有提到孩子們？我們不能在晚上單獨留下孩子們啊！

Receptionist

Mrs. Foreman, the housekeeper will arrange for a reliable woman to sit with them.
福門太太，房務管理員會替您安排可靠的保母來照顧他們的。

Mr. Foreman Would you please ask the housekeeper as soon as possible?
請你通知房務管理員儘快給我們找保母好嗎？

Receptionist Thank you, sir. We are always glad to help you.
謝謝您，先生。為您服務是我們的光榮。

- Visitor　訪客。

- pleasantly　愉快的、快樂的。

- just now　剛剛、剛才。

- hand to　交給、遞給。

- note　便箋、摘要。

- listen　聽著、聆聽。

- welcome　歡迎。

- fair city　美麗的城市。

- dinner　晚餐、正式的宴會。

- hurry　快、急。

- locate　找出、找到。

- beauty parlor　美容院。

- nearby　附近的。

- mezzanine　夾層樓、中層樓。

- stairway　樓梯。

- turn　轉彎。

- suppose　推測、猜想。

- barber shop　理髮廳。

- sauna bath　三溫暖、蒸氣浴、芬蘭浴。

- idea　意見、想法、構想。

- clothes　衣服。

- pressing　燙，衣服要燙。

- valet　洗衣部門的人員。

- immediate service　立即服務、快速交件。

- wear 穿著、穿戴。
- alone 單獨的、一個人的。
- arrange 安排、整理。
- reliable woman 可靠的女傭。
- take care of 照顧。

house maids 客房女清潔員

028

Receptionist　Mr. William, how are you today?
威廉先生，您今天好嗎？

Mr. William　Fine thanks, and you?
很好，謝謝，你好嗎？

Receptionist　Not so well. I'm certainly glad to see you.
不很好。但我很高興見到您。

Mr. William　Yes, what can I do for you?
是的，我能幫你什麼忙嗎？

Receptionist　Well. It's like this. You remember your wealthy friend, Mr. Cook, who always stayed here at least a week or more every month, don't you?
是這樣的。您記得您那位有錢的朋友，古克先生嗎？他每個月起碼住在這裡一個星期或更長，還記得嗎？

Mr. William　Oh! Yes, didn't you...
哦！是的，你不…

Receptionist　You remember how elegantly he dressed and what expensive cuff links, watch and diamond stick pin he always wore, don't you?
您記得他的衣著是多麼的高雅吧！並經常穿戴高貴的袖扣、手錶、鑽石別針，不是嗎？

Mr. William　Yes, his....
是的，他的……

Receptionist　And we always gave him a large suite and the best service.
我們每次都給他一間大的套房以及最好的服務。

Mr. William Oh, yes, only the best for old Cook. But let me...
哦！是的，只有給老古克最好的，而讓我⋯⋯

Receptionist I believe his last reservation a week ago was made by you, wasn't it?
我記得他上次的訂房，是一星期前由您訂的，不是嗎？

Mr. William I suppose so. He usually called me to reserve a room. But didn't you...
我想大概是吧。他經常要我給他訂房。但你不⋯⋯

Receptionist You remember when he was here last, don't you? He was more extravagant than before. He always entertained a lot of people. But last week he gave a big cocktail party in his room. His bar bill alone was more than my monthly salary.
您記得他上次住在這裡的時候，比以前更浪費，他以前經常招待很多的人。上星期在他的房裡，舉行盛大的酒會。他的酒帳就已超過我的一個月薪水了。

Mr. William There's nothing cheap about Cook. He entertains like a king and spends money like a millionaire. However, I don't like him. But yet...
對老古克來說，沒有便宜的東西。他招待客人就像國王一樣，他花錢也像是百萬富翁。我不喜歡他這種做法，不過，還是⋯⋯

Receptionist But I always thought that he was a millionaire. His long distance calls are in the four figures. Here is his last bill.
我總以為他是百萬富翁。他的長途電話費是四位數的（上千的）。這是他上次的帳單。

Mr. William Whew! This is the biggest bill that I've ever seen. I've never seen one like this. But don't...
哇！我從來沒見過，這麼大數字的帳單。我也沒見過像這樣的人。但我不⋯⋯

Receptionist

I haven't either. And you know I seldom take a personal check from anyone, and I never give credit. But I trusted him. He has always paid on a credit card. But this time I allowed him to pay by check. Now, look at this. It's a letter from his bank. His check was returned. It says "Lack of funds."

我也沒見過。您知道我很少接受私人支票的，我也沒有背書過。不過我相信他。他一向是以信用卡付帳的。而這次我特准以支票付帳。現在，你看！這是他銀行來的信。被退票了，「無法兌現」。

Mr. William

Well, as we say "Easy come; easy go." But don't worry, I've been trying to tell you that it's all right. Send the check back to the bank. Mr.Cook is a rich man now. His uncle died yesterday and left him an oilfield in Alaska.

好吧，就像我們說的「容易來；容易去」，不過不必擔心，我想錢是沒有問題的，你把支票寄回銀行，古克先生現在是有錢人了，他的叔叔昨天去世，留下了阿拉斯加的一片油田。

- receptionist 接待員。
- wealthy 富有的。
- at least 至少。
- elegantly 高雅。
- diamond stick pin 鑽石別針。
- large suite 大套房。
- best service 最好的服務。
- made by you 由你訂的（房間）、你經手的。
- extravagant 浪費；慣於浪費。
- entertain 招待（吃喝的），請客。
- cocktail party 雞尾酒會。
- more than 超過。
- king 國王。
- millionaire 百萬富翁。
- four figures 四位數字。
- cuff links 袖口扣針。
- biggest 最大的。
- ever seen 見過的。
- seldom 很少。
- personal check 私人的支票。
- give credit 背書。
- trust 信任。
- paid 已付（帳）。
- allow 准許。

- pay　付（款）。
- bank　銀行。
- check was returned　被退票了。
- Lack of fund　戶頭沒有錢；支票無法兌現。
- as we say　如我們所說的。
- Easy come, easy go.　容易來，容易去。來得容易，去得快。
- all right　沒問題。

(Mr. Foreman has taken the telephone off the hook.)
（福門先生拿起電話筒。）

Telephone operator

Good evening, Mr. Foreman. May I help you?
晚安，福門先生。我能為您效勞嗎？

Mr. Foreman

You certainly can. How about being our alarm clock?
你當然可以，可以當我們的鬧鐘嗎？

Telephone operator

With pleasure. We are used to interrupting people's sleep.
沒問題！我們習慣打斷人家的睡眠。

Mr. Foreman

O.K. Then, please wake us up early tomorrow morning. We have to catch a plane at seven o'clock. Will you call us at six?
好的。請你明天一早叫我們起床。我們要趕七點鐘的飛機，請妳六點叫我們好嗎？

Telephone operator

You're taking an international flight, aren't you?
您是不是要搭乘國際班機？

Mr. Foreman

Yes, we're going home.
是的，我們要回家了。

Telephone operator

For international flights passengers have to be at the airport two hours early. I think you ought to get up a little earlier than five.
搭乘國際班機的旅客，必需要在二小時前到達機場。我想您還是五點以前起床較好。

(034)

Mr. Foreman

Oh, yes. I forgot about that. How long does it take to get to the airport from here?
哦！是的，我忘了。這裡到機場多遠？

At that time in the morning it shouldn't take much more than forty minutes and surely less than an hour.

在早上那段時間不會超過四十分鐘，最多不會超過一小時。

You had better give us a call at four o'clock sharp. The children are slow in the morning. They take more time to get ready. It will be dark at that time, too.

我想還是四點準時叫我們比較好。孩子們都起得較慢，而且要多些時間來準備。那時天也還沒亮。

I believe I ought to call you at four o'clock.

我想我應該在四點叫您。

O.K. if you say so. By the way, send up a pot of strong coffee, please, and hot chocolate for the three children.

好吧，就這樣吧！順便請人送一壺濃的咖啡，和三份熱巧克力來，好嗎？

I'll call room service right away and you may place your order with them. You'll be served breakfast on the plane, won't you?

我接客房餐飲部給您，您跟他們叫好了。飛機上不是也有早餐嗎？

I suppose so. We'll miss the special food of this country.

我想有吧！我們將會錯過這裡的特別餐點了。

Yes, indeed. Will there be anything else?

是啊，還有其他吩咐嗎？

Mr. Foreman

Not now. Thanks for telling us about those stores. However, I ought not to thank you. My wife has spent all my money. By the way, will you call her now, please? She's at the Beauty Parlor. What time is it now?

沒有了。謝謝妳介紹那些商店給我們，不過也不該謝妳，我的錢都被我太太花光了。順便請妳打個電話給她，她在美容院。現在幾點鐘了？

Telephone operator

It's exactly five minutes to six. I'll connect you with the Beauty Parlor. Hold on, please.

正好五點五十五分。請等一下，我給您接美容院。

・說明：國際五星級飯店，大部份採用電腦系統，旅客自行設定叫醒時間，無需經話務員叫醒。若無此設施者，才由話務員叫醒。

- telephone operator　接線員、話務員。
- morning call　晨間叫醒。
- hook　聽筒（電話）。
- alarm clock　鬧鐘。
- interrupt　打斷。
- wake up　叫醒。
- to catch a plane　要趕飛機。
- international flight　國際班機。
- passenger　乘客（車、船、飛機等）。
- ought to　應該。
- forgot　忘了。
- how long　要多少時間、多遠。
- at that time　在那個時間（時刻）。
- more than　超過。
- surely　一定的。
- less than　少於、不會超過。
- sharp　準時，與on time相同。
- ready　準備。
- an hour early　提前一個小時。
- dark　天未亮；黑暗。
- if you say so　就如你說的、照你說的。
- arrive　到達。
- by the way　順便。
- pot　壺（裝飲料的容器）。

- strong coffee　濃濃的咖啡。
- hot chocolate　熱的巧克力。
- serve breakfast　提供早餐、招待早餐。
- on the plane　在飛機上。
- miss　錯過；想念。
- special food　具有特色的菜餚。
- indeed　的確。
- anything else　還有什麼吩咐。
- not now　現在沒有。

Mr. Foreman

Operator, I want to place an international call to Los Angeles, please. Are there special night rates from here?

接線員，請你幫我打個國際電話到洛杉磯，現在起是否以夜間費用計算呢？

Telephone operator

Yes, the night rates are from nine in the evening until seven in the morning.

是的，夜間費用的計算是從晚上九點到明早的七點止。

Mr. Foreman

What time is it in Los Angeles?

洛山磯現在是什麼時間？（意即與本地的時差是多少。）

Telephone operator

There is a time difference of fifteen hours.

與本地的時差是15小時。

Mr. Foreman

Fine, I'd like to put a call in now.

好的，現在就幫我打吧！

Telephone operator

Wait a minute please. I'll connect you with international call operator.

請等一下，我幫您接國際台。

Mr. Foreman

Could you make the call for me? I speak only English. I used to speak Chinese, but I don't any more.

你幫我打好嗎？我只會說英語，我以前會說華語，但現在都忘了。

Telephone operator

All international call operators speak English, sir.

先生，所有國際台的接線員都會說英語的。

Mr. Foreman

But I don't want the call put on my bill. I want to charge it to my credit card.

電話費不要加入我的旅館帳目內，我要用信用卡付帳。

Telephone operator

What is the number of your card?

您的信用卡號碼幾號？

Mr. Foreman

It's 3812-112266-006, Diners Club International.

戴拿斯（大來）信用卡，卡號3812-112266-006。

Telephone operator

Thank you, sir. I'll get international call and report the charges to you later.

謝謝您，先生。我幫您接國際台，等會兒告訴您要多少費用。

Mr. Foreman

Can I get the call through right away?

是否可以立即接通呢？

Telephone operator

I think so. But if the circuits are busy, you may have to wait a little while.

我想可以，但是假如線路忙的話，您也許要等一下。

Telephone operator

Just a minute, please. I have international call now. Hold on. Overseas call, Mr. Foreman, room 1502 of the Taipei Hotel, wants to place a international call. He wants to charge it to his credit card.

請等一下，國際台接通了，請不要掛斷。國際台，這裡是臺北大飯店，1502號房的福門先生要打國際電話，以信用卡付帳。

Overseas call operator

Who do you want to call, Mr. Foreman?

您要打給誰，福門先生？

Mr. Foreman

I'd like to put in a station-to-station call to Los Angeles, area code 213, number 683-1234. Charge it to my credit card. (Mr. Foreman repeats his credit card number.)

我要叫號，洛杉磯，區號213，電話號碼是683-1234。費用

列入我的信用卡內（福門先生又重念了他的信用卡號碼）。

Overseas call operator

Hang up, please. I'll call you back in a few minutes. (The international call operator called back fifteen minutes later. Allen answers the telephone.)
請掛斷，我在幾分鐘內給您回答。（十五分鐘後，國際台接線員回電，愛倫接聽。）

Overseas call operator

Here is your party in Los Angeles, Mr. Foreman.
福門先生，您打到洛杉磯的電話接通了。

Mr. Foreman

Fine, thanks.
好的，謝謝。

‧說明：國際五星級飯店，大部份採用全球通訊系統，設定國碼Country Code／區域號碼Area Code／直撥對方電話號碼／自動入帳。但是有些旅客還是喜歡由總機接線員轉接。

- international call　國際電話。
- to place　掛接（電話）。
- night rate　夜間計費（電話）。
- time difference　時差。
- to put a call　撥一通電話。
- connect with　接⋯。
- overseas call operator　國際台接線生。
- used to　曾經。
- put on 計算在……。
- charge　費用。
- credit card　信用卡。
- Diners Club International　信用卡公司名稱。台灣稱為「大來信用卡」。
- report the charge　回報（電話）費用。
- I think so　我想是的。
- circuits　（電話）迴路。
- station-to-station　叫號的電話。
- person-to-person　叫人電話。
- local call　市內電話。
- area code　地區號碼。
- Hang up, please.　請掛上（電話筒）。
- call you back　回您電話。
- your party　對方，聽電話的人。
- night club　夜總會。
- through　經過、通過。

9. Emergency call 緊急電話 ⊙ 1-1-9

Receptionist Dr. Mc.! Dr. Mc, please wait! A man in room 1818 has just reported that he heard someone groaning and moaning in room 1820. Our old guest, Mr. Miller, occupies that room, Will you please go up with me to see if he is all right?

麥醫生！麥醫生，請等一下！剛剛1818的房客說，他聽到有人在1820房間內呻吟、哭泣。那個房間住的是老顧客米樂先生。請您和我一道上去看看是否有什麼問題好嗎？

Dr. Mc. I'll go if you think he's really sick. You know, of course, that I do not have a license to practice medicine in this country. But I can tell you whether the man is ill.

如果你認為他真的是生病的話，我和你一道去。你知道，我沒有在這裡行醫的執照。但我可以告訴你，他患的是什麼病。

Receptionist Good. Let's see what the trouble is. Do you have your medical bag?

好的。我們看看到底是出了什麼問題。您有帶醫療包嗎？

Receptionist Mr. Miller, Mr. Miller, can you hear me?

米樂先生，米樂先生，您聽見了沒有？

Mr. Miller Oh, the pain. (Dr. Mc. quickly examines him.)

哦！好痛（麥醫生立即給他檢查）。

Dr. Mc. Call an ambulance immediately. His appendix is very bad. I'll go with him to the hospital. Will you write out a permit for his admittance and assume responsibility for payment?

立刻叫救護車。急性盲腸炎。我送他到醫院。你寫一張住院證明以及保證負責費用好嗎？

Receptionist

Yes, indeed. He is an old guest of ours, a very fine man. The ambulance is on the way. I'll have to notify his family. Is he in a very serious condition, Doctor?

好的。他是我們的老主顧，是一位好人。救護車已經開出來了。我會通知他的家屬。他是否很嚴重啊，醫生？

Dr. Mc.

I don't know exactly how dangerous it is now, but I believe he'll have to have an emergency operation. Is the hospital far from here?

現在我還不十分明確瞭解他有多危險，不過，我相信他需要緊急手術。醫院遠不遠？

Receptionist

No, it's straight ahead, five blocks up the street, then west about three blocks. It's on the corner. As soon as he leaves. I'll have the maid pack his clothes and clean the room. She'll change the mattress and put on clean linen. The room will be ready for you when you return, Doctor.

不遠，就在前面，過五條街轉西再過三條街。就在轉角的地方。他一走立即叫清潔員收拾他的衣服，然後把房間打掃乾淨，換床墊、床單。當您回來時，這個房間給您住。

Dr. Mc.

It's too bad that we have to send a man to the hospital so that I can get a room. Meanwhile, please pull the drapes and curtains and open the window. We need fresh air in here.

真不幸！要送這位病人到醫院，我才有一間房間住。請把窗簾拉開，窗子打開。這裡需要新鮮空氣。

Receptionist

You certainly arrived at the right time, Doctor.

您的確來得正是時候呀！醫生。

- emergency call　緊急電話。
- moan　呻吟。
- groan　哭泣。
- sick　病的。
- license　執照。
- practice　執業（醫師的）。
- medicine　醫藥（醫學）。
- ill　生病的。
- medical bag　醫護包。
- lying on　躺在。
- hear　聽。
- pain　痛。
- examine　診療。
- ambulance　救護車。
- immediately　立即。
- appendix　本文指盲腸之意。
- hospital　醫院。
- permit　准許、許可。
- admittance　住院。
- responsibility　負責。
- payment　付款、款項、費用。
- old client/guest　老顧客。
- carry out　實行、完成。
- doctor's order　醫師的要求（指示）。

- on the way　在路上。

- notify　通知、告知。

- serious condition　情況嚴重。

- dangerous　危險。

- emergency operation　緊急開刀（手術）。

- straight ahead　直行；前面。

- corner　轉角。

- block　一區（街道的）。

- pack　包、捆。

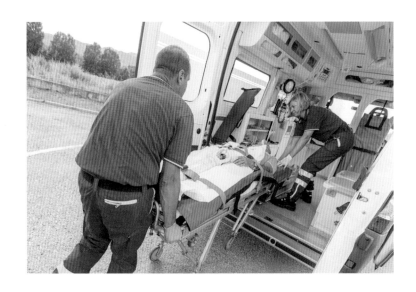

Mr. Winner
Hi! You're looking lovely this morning. How's everything?
嗨！妳今早氣色真好，一切都順利嗎？

P. R. director
Fine, thanks. You Americans arrive on time, don't you? It's only a quarter past eight.When did you get up?
很好，謝謝。你們美國人很守時，不是嗎？現在才八點十五分。你幾點起床的？

Mr. Winner
I'll tell you when I got up, but don't ask me when I went to bed. This is a lovely town at night, isn't it?
我會告訴妳，我什麼時候起床，但是不要問我，什麼時候上床。這個城市的夜色真迷人，不是嗎？

P. R. director
People say it is. How long are you staying here?
大家都這麼說。你打算在這裡逗留多久？

Mr. Winner
Unfortunately I can stay only for a few days. I arrived the day before yesterday, May 20th, and I'll leave May 24th. I've been traveling for three months.
很遺憾，我只能住幾天而已。我是前天，五月二十日到的，我將在五月廿四日離開。我已經出來旅行三個月了。

P. R. director
That's a long time. Come. We have work to do. How about beginning at the bottom of the hotel and going to the top? Would you like to see the laundry with its modern equipment? The kitchen, with its new stoves and refrigerators, may inter-est some people. It's nice and clean there. You can take a photograph of the French chef with his tall

white cap, working among his pots and pans. Perhaps he will take one of his famous soufflés for you.

是一段滿長的時間。我們工作吧！從底下開始往上走吧。你喜歡看看現代化設備的洗衣房嗎？廚房，有新的爐灶、冰箱，也許有些人對此有興趣。那裡很乾淨，你可以給戴著高高白帽，在瓶罐、鍋子間工作的法國主廚拍張照片。也許他會請你嚐嚐他拿手的「蛋白牛奶酥」呢！

Mr. Winner

I could eat one now, because I haven't had breakfast yet. I think this side entrance with its pretty shops—the dress shops, the flower shop, and jewelry shops—would make an attractive picture. The travel bureau, car rental agency, and bookstores should interest clients, too.

我可以現在吃，因為我還沒吃早餐。這入口是到商店街的吧！──洋裝店、花店、珠寶店，可以拍一張迷人的照片。旅行社、租車店、書店，顧客對這些也是有興趣的。

P. R. director

And also the art gallery here, near the corridor. First look at the pictures in my files. You may like some of them.

藝廊也在這裡靠走廊的地方。先看看我檔案裡的照片，有些你可能會喜歡。

Mr. Winner

Oh, these pictures of the bars, with the barmaids and bartenders and entertainers, are great. They'll bring in the customers.

哦！這些酒吧的照片有女服務員、調酒員、藝人，很棒！他（她）們會吸引顧客的。

P. R. director

O.K. Do you like these of the restaurants with the waiters and waitresses?

好的。這些是餐廳的照片，有男女服務員，你喜歡嗎？

Mr. Winner

Yes, their costumes are attractive. Can you lend me a few of these photographs? Some of these color pictures of the garden, the terrace, and the swimming pool are very pretty.

是的，他（她）的服裝很迷人。這些照片妳可以借我幾張嗎？這些花園、台階、游泳池的彩色照片非常美麗。

P. R. director Here's one Miss Anne Murray, the movie star, near the pool.

站在游泳池邊的，是電影明星安妮‧木蕾小姐。

Mr. Winner Fine. Pictures must be taken of the manager, his staff, and particularly one of the P.R. director.

很好。還要拍經理、職員，特別是公共關係經理的照片。

- look lovely 看起來很可愛。
- P. R. director 公關經理。
- on time 準時。
- get up 起床、起來。
- people say it is 人人都這樣說。
- beginning 起先、開始。
- bottom 底、根基。
- top 上端；上座。
- laundry 洗衣。
- equipment 設備。
- kitchen 廚房。
- stove 火爐、爐灶。
- refrigerator 冰箱。
- French chef 法國廚師。
- pan 平底鍋、淺鍋。
- famous 著名、出名。
- souffles 蛋白牛奶酥。
- dress shop 女裝店。
- flower shop 鮮花店。
- jewelry shop 珠寶店。
- attractive 有魅力的、吸引人的。
- travel bureau 旅行社。
- car rental agency 租車店。
- book store 書店。

- client　顧客。
- art gallery　藝廊。
- corridor　走廊、迴廊。
- file　檔案。
- barmaid　酒吧服務員（女性）。
- bartender　調酒員。
- are great　大的；太好了。
- bring in　帶進；介紹。
- customer　顧客、主顧。
- restaurant　餐廳。
- waiter　服務員（男性）。
- waitress　服務員（女性）。
- costume　服裝。
- garden　花園。
- movie　電影。
- star　星星；明星。
- particularly　特別地；格外；詳細地。
- pot　深底鍋；壺。
- rear entrance　後門。
- side entrance　側門、邊門。
- golf course　高爾夫球場。
- tennis court　網球場。

洗手間

TOILET	男女分開
LAVATORY	男女分開
MEN'S ROOM	限男用
LADIE'S ROOM	限女用
WASH ROOM	限女用
POWDER ROOM	限女用
WATER CLOSET (W.C.)	男女分開
REST ROOM	男女分開

Mr. Foreman
Operator, this is Mr. Foreman in 1502, I want to speak to the manager right away.
接線員，我是1502號房的福門先生，我現在要和經理講話。

Telephone operator
Yes. Mr. Foreman... I'm sorry. The manager's line is busy. I'll call you back when it is free. (In three minutes she calls Mr. Foreman.) I'm ringing Mr. Pan's office for you, Mr. Foreman.
是的，福門先生……對不起，經理正在講話中，講完了我給您接過來。（三分鐘內她接給福門先生）我接潘先生的辦公室給您，福門先生。

Secretary
(Answers the phone.) Mr. Pan's office, who's calling, please?
（回答電話）這裡是潘先生的辦公室，請問貴姓？

Mr. Foreman
Mr. Foreman in 1502. I want to speak to Mr. Pan.
我是1502房的福門先生，我要和潘先生講話。

Secretary
I'm sorry, Mr. Foreman. Mr. Pan is not in his office now. Would you like to speak to Mr. Chang, the assistant manager?
對不起，福門先生。潘先生此刻不在辦公室，您要不要和副經理張先生談呢？

Mr. Foreman
No, I must speak to Mr. Pan personally. Isn't he in the hotel?
不，我一定要和潘先生親自談，他沒離開旅館吧？

Secretary
Just a minute, Mr. Foreman. I'll try to locate him. Hold on. Don't hang up.
請等一下，福門先生，我找找看，不要掛斷。

Mr. Pan (On the telephone.) This is Pan... speaking.
（轉接電話）我姓潘。

Mr. Foreman Mr. Pan, this is Foreman in 1502. I have some bad news to report.
潘先生，我是1502房的福門，我有些壞消息要告訴您。

Mr. Pan Oh? What is the news, Mr. Foreman?

哦？是什麼消息啊！福門先生？

Mr. Foreman It's a rainy day, and the boys were staying in their room. They have colds and can't go out.
這個下雨天，二個男孩要留在他們房間裡，因為他們都感冒了，所以不能出去。

Mr. Pan Oh, that's too bad. It's nothing serious, I hope.
哦，太糟了！我希望不會是很嚴重吧！

Mr. Foreman Well, it's serious enough. While Mrs. Foreman, Nancy, and I were out, the boys broke a window, a mirror above the dresser, and a lamp beside the bed. They were playing ball, I guess. Can you get a repairman to fix the window and someone to clean the room? There is a lot of glass on the rug.
是的，相當嚴重。我們夫婦和女兒出去的時間裡，孩子們打破一塊窗子及梳妝臺上的鏡子，還有床邊的檯燈也打壞了。我猜他們是在房間裡打球的吧！請您叫人來修理窗子和打掃房間好嗎？地毯上有很多的破玻璃碎片。

Mr. Pan Yes, Mr. Foreman. I'll inform the maintenance department and the housekeeper. Thank you for calling.
好的，福門先生。我會通知養護部和房務人員。謝謝您的電話。

Mr. Foreman I'm very sorry. I'll pay for the damage, of course. The responsibility is mine. Usually the boys behave quite well.
非常抱歉，我會負責賠償這些損壞，孩子一向都很守規矩的！

Mr. Pan Don't worry, Mr. Foreman. Boys will be boys.
不要擔心，福門先生。男孩總是男孩。

- Room damage　損壞設備（客房）。
- telephone operator　電話接線員、話務員。
- speak to　跟……說話。
- line is busy　電話佔線／講話中。
- free　不佔線。
- ringing　電話鈴響。
- secretary　秘書。
- who's　是誰。
- personally　親自的、個人的。
- hold on　等一下（電話的）。
- don't hang up　不要掛斷。
- report　報告。
- have a cold　受涼、感冒。
- serious　嚴重。
- serious enough　很嚴重。
- window　窗子。
- mirror　鏡子。
- dresser　梳妝臺。
- guess　猜想。
- rug　地毯（鋪一部份）。carpet地毯（全鋪）。
- maintenance department　修護部。
- responsibility　責任。
- usually　平常、通常。
- behave　表現。
- don't worry　不要擔心、放心。

Housekeeper

The maid just gave me this little locket. She found it under the bed in suite 1502. The occupants have checked out.

剛剛清潔員給我這個小紀念盒。她在1502號房的床下發現的，房客已經遷出了。

Receptionist

That's pretty. Let's see who occupied that suite. Oh yes, the Foreman's and their three children. They left about an hour ago, I believe. (She opens the locket.) Here is a picture of a little girl. Yes, that is Mr. Foreman's daughter.

好美啊！我看看那間套房是誰住的。哦！是福門一家人，他們走了約有一小時了。（她打開盒子）有一個小女孩的相片。對，她就是福門先生的女兒。

(The telephone rings.)
（電話鈴響。）

Mr. Foreman

Hello, is that the information desk?
喂，是詢問台嗎？

Receptionist

Yes, it is, sir. What may I do for you?
是的，先生。有什麼事要我效勞的嗎？

Mr. Foreman

This is Mr. Billy Foreman. I just checked out of suite 1502.
我是比利福門，我剛剛由1502號套房遷出的。

Receptionist

Yes, Mr. Foreman. Good morning. How are you this morning?
是的，福門先生，早安。您好嗎？

Mr. Foreman

I don't feel very well myself. I've caught a cold. But my little girl feels worse than I do. She has lost her locket. I wonder if she left it in her room. Perhaps she dropped it some place in the hotel.

我自己覺得不很好，我感冒了。我的小女兒的心情比我更糟。她掉了一個小紀念盒，我懷疑是掉在她的房裡，或是掉在旅館其他地方。

Receptionist

Mr. Foreman, your little girl is lucky. A locket was found by the maid and was given to me just now. I'm sure it is the one your daughter lost. It has her picture inside.

福門先生，您的小女兒真幸運。那個小紀念盒被清潔員撿到，她剛剛交給我，這個就是您女兒遺失的沒錯，裡面有她的照片。

Mr. Foreman

Oh good! Nancy will be very happy. It was given to her on her last birthday. How can we get it? They are announcing our flight now.

哦，好極了！南西一定會很高興。那是去年她的生日禮物。我們怎麼去拿呢？班機就要起飛了。

Receptionist

We have your home address. Mr. Foreman. We'll send it to you today.

福門先生，我們有您家的住址。今天就寄給您。

Mr. Foreman

That's very kind of you. I'll tell my friends about your hotel. We have had very good service. We will always remember what you have done. Let me know the postal charges, and I'll send you a check.

你們實在太親切了。我要告訴我的朋友，有關你們旅館的親切服務。我們得到這麼好的服務，我們永遠記在心裡。告訴我多少郵資，我會寄支票給你。

Receptionist

Don't worry about that, Mr. Foreman. We're glad to do that for you. The locket will be taken to the post office today and sent registered mail to you. Have a nice trip home.

不要擔心那些，福門先生，這是我們應該做的事。小
紀念盒今天就以掛號寄去給您，祝您旅途愉快。

Mr. Foreman　Thanks a lot. We won't forget your courtesy. Oh,
by the way, I found a key to one of the rooms in
my pocket.
非常謝謝。我們不會忘記你對我們的好意。哦！我發
現有一把鑰匙在我口袋裡。

Receptionist　Just drop it in the mailbox in the airport, and we'll
get it. The name of the hotel is on the tag of every
key.
丟入機場的郵筒就可以了。鑰匙把上有旅館的名字，
我們會收到的。

Mr. Foreman　I'll do that now. Good-bye.
我會丟入郵筒的。再見！

maids truck　　*客房清潔推車*

- housekeeper　房務管理員。
- lost and found　失物招領。
- locket　金屬做的紀念品小盒。
- found　發現。
- under the bed　床的底下。
- occupant　住用者、住的人。
- picture　照片。
- little girl　小女孩。
- daughter　女兒。
- caught a cold　感冒、傷風。
- inside　裡面。
- get it　拿到。
- announcing　廣播中。
- home address　住家地址。
- sent　郵寄。
- kind of　親切。
- postal charge　郵資。
- glad to　高興的。
- post office　郵局。
- registered mail　掛號郵件。
- courtesy　禮貌；好意。
- mailbox　郵筒、郵箱。
- tag　標籤。
- key tag　掛鑰匙的標牌。

Miss Hana
Listen, Mr. Pan. I have a complaint.
潘先生，我要向你抱怨。

Mr. Pan/manager
Who is speaking, please?
請問您是哪位？

Miss Hana
Hana is my name. And I haven't slept all night.
我的名字叫漢娜。我整個晚上都沒睡好。

Mr. Pan/manager
I'm very sorry, Miss Hana. Aren't you feeling well?
很抱歉，漢娜小姐。您覺得好些了嗎？

Miss Hana
I'm not feeling well, either. I put a "Do Not Disturb" sign on my door last night, and it didn't do any good. I've been disturbed all night.
我覺得很不舒服，昨晚我把「請勿打擾」的牌子掛在門把上，也一樣沒有用。我整個晚上都被打擾。

Mr. Pan/manager
Please tell me what happened, Miss Hana.
請告訴我，是怎麼一回事，漢娜小姐。

Miss Hana
The people in the next room, 1604, have been making so much noise that I haven't been able to sleep.
我隔壁的1604號房，整晚都很吵，我實在無法入睡。

Mr. Pan/manager
That's too bad. Nobody else reported a disturbance. Tell me what they did.
那太糟了。怎麼沒有其他人報告吵嚷的事。到底他們怎麼吵的。

Miss Hana
There was a lot of singing and shouting.
他們一直在唱歌、吶喊。

Mr. Pan/manager Why haven't you reported the disturbance before, Miss Hana?
為什麼在吵的時候您不說呢？漢娜小姐。

Miss Hana Well, you weren't here.
那時你不在呀！

Mr. Pan/manager I'm sorry, but the security has been on duty all night. They received no complaints. How long are you staying?
很抱歉，但是我的警衛人員整晚都在值班的。他們並沒有接到不滿的報告。您要住多久？

Miss Hana Since I can't rest, I'm going to leave soon. I'll pack up my clothes when I feel better, but I'm feeling worse. While I am lying in bed here trying to sleep, the lady across the way is annoying me.
我得不到休息，我只好快點搬了。等我感到舒服些時，我將收拾衣服。不過我的精神很差。我躺在床上想睡時，有一位女士走過來打擾了我。

Mr. Pan/manager What lady? Across what way? In what room? I would like to know how she is annoying you.
什麼女士？走過哪裡？在哪號房間？我想知道她是怎樣吵您的。

Miss Hana In front of my window is a young lady in a bikini, taking a sun bath on the terrace. I can't sleep.
就在我窗子的前面，有一位年輕的小姐穿著比基尼泳裝，在台階上做日光浴，我睡不著。

Mr. Pan/manager I have a remedy, Miss Hana. Close your blinds.
我有藥方，漢娜小姐，把您的眼睛閉上就好了。

062

- complaint 抱怨。
- Do Not Disturb (DND) 不要打擾。
- next room 隔壁房。
- noise 噪音，不安靜。
- sing 唱歌。
- security 警衛。
- on duty 值班。
- nervous 神經過敏，神經質的。
- leave 離開。
- bikini 比基尼泳裝。
- sun bath 日光浴。
- terrace 庭園的台階、陽台、梯形的台階。
- remedy 藥方、治療法。
- blind 閉上眼睛。
- Mak up room, please. 請打掃（整理）房間。
- shout 大聲喊叫。

Mr. Foreman
Good evening. We're going to leave early tomorrow morning. Will you please prepare my bill?
晚安。我們明天一早就要離開,請你準備我的帳單好嗎?

Cashier
Yes, indeed, Mr. Foreman. We'll have your statement ready in the morning. You are in suite 1502, aren't you?
是的,福門先生。明早我們會把明細表做好給您的,您是1502號套房對嗎?

Mr. Foreman
That's right. Can you tell me how much it is now?
是的。你能告訴我目前是多少錢嗎?

Cashier
Of course, I'll get your account right away. Here it is, Mr. Foreman. This is the amount up to this time. There will be a few other items to add today, I guess.
當然可以,我立刻算算看。這裡就是,福門先生,這是到現在為止的金額,不過我想今天還有一些要加上去的。

Mr. Foreman
Well, I'd like to know the bad news now. (He looks over the bills and checks his signatures.) This looks like our national debt. It's worse than I thought. Let me figure it out. What's the date today?
好的,現在我要面對壞消息了。(他看看帳單並核對簽名)這個看起來好像是我們的國際貸款(意即數目相當大),比我想像中更糟,讓我算算,今天是幾號啊?

Cashier
It's the twenty of November. You have been here for two weeks. There are five in your family, and you have charged a lot of meals. There are orders from room service and from the valet. There's the cost of the window and mirror, and also TV.
今天是11月20號。您住了二個星期,一家五位,許多由客房餐飲送來的用餐帳單及洗衣服的帳單,另外還有賠償窗

子、鏡子、電視機的錢。

Mrs. Foreman
And there are a few bills from the bar also.
還有幾張帳單是酒吧送來的。

Mr. Foreman
I'm not complaining. But this is the highest bill I've ever got. How much is it in U.S. dollars?
我不是在抱怨。這是我付過帳中最多的一次，折合多少美金？

Cashier
That's exactly six thousand two hundred eighty dollars.
正好是六千二百八十元。

Mr. Foreman
(To Mrs. Foreman) Well, we certainly won't celebrate tonight.
（面對福門太太）好了，今晚無法慶祝一番了。（意思是說錢都花光了。）

Mrs. Foreman
Things here are as expensive as they are at home.
這裡的東西和我們那裡的一樣貴。

Mr. Foreman
I'll settle in full before we leave in the morning. We have to catch an early plane.
明早在我離開前會全部付清，我們要趕早班的飛機。

Cashier
Will you pay with traveler's checks or with a credit card?
您是用旅行支票或信用卡付帳？

Mr. Foreman
I'll have to use my credit card. We have spent all the traveler's checks.
我們的旅行支票全都花光了，我只好用信用卡付帳了。

Cashier
I hope you have enjoyed your visit here with us.
希望您在此渡假期間玩得愉快。

Mrs. Foreman　Indeed we have. This was the most wonderful vacation that we have ever had. We are planning to return next year.

是的。這是一次非常難忘的假期。我們計劃明年再來。

Mr. Foreman　Yes, everything was first class. The suite was fine, the air conditioner and showers worked, the beds were comfortable, and the service and food were very good.

是的，全都是一流的。套房不錯，空氣調節及淋浴蓮蓬頭都很好用，床也舒適，服務及餐點都很好。

Cashier　Splendid. Let us know when you are coming next year. We'll send up champagne with the roses. Wait a minute. I'll tell Mr. Pan that you are leaving. He will want to say good-bye to you. Have a good trip to Los Angeles.

謝謝您的稱讚。讓我們知道明年什麼時候再來，我們將送香檳酒及玫瑰花給您。請等一下，我來告訴潘先生說您就要回去了。他要和您說再見，祝您快樂的回到洛杉磯。

- check-out　結帳退房。
- prepare my bill　準備我的帳單。
- statement　明細表。
- up to this time　到現在為止。
- item(s)　項目。
- add　加入、加上。
- signature　簽名。
- national debt　國際貸款。
- worse　壞。
- thought　想像。
- figure　計算。
- meal(s)　餐點。
- bar　酒吧。
- highest　最高的。
- celebrate　慶祝。
- expensive　（花費的）貴。
- settle in full　全部付清。
- wonderful vacation　美妙假期。
- first class　頭等、一流的。
- air conditioner　空氣調節器。
- comfortable　舒適、舒服。
- splendid　上等的、極好的。
- champagne　香檳。
- rose　薔薇、玫瑰。
- say good-bye to you　向您說聲再見。
- have a good trip　祝您一路平安。

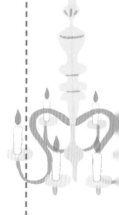

二、從業人員

Walk-in guest　Good evening. I want to cash a traveler's check. I'm going to buy a few things in the shops here. I'd like the money in local currency instead of dollars, please. What is the rate of exchange today?
晚安。我的旅行支票想換成現金，買些東西。我想把它換為本地的錢幣，不知道今天的匯率是多少？

Cashier　It is NT$ thirty per dollar. There is a small service charge. May I see your passport or identification, please?
一美元對換新台幣三十元，另加一些服務費，您的護照或身分證，讓我看看好嗎？

Walk-in guest　(Searching with his left hand in all his pockets.) Oh, dear. I did not bring it. I changed my suit and left my passport and other things in my room.
（他用左手找遍了他所有的口袋）哦！我忘了帶，我換西裝後把護照及一些證件都留在房間裡了。

Cashier　This is the first check in your book. You haven't cashed any other checks yet.
這是第一張支票，你還沒有兌換過呢！（book是指整本的支票。）

Walk-in guest　No, this is the first one.
還沒換過，這是第一張。

Cashier　Just a minute, please. (Cashier calls the front desk and asks if Mr. Billy Foreman is registered. The receptionist replies that Mr. Billy Foreman occupies suite 1502. He also says that the Foremans were going to the beach for

(068)

a couple of days but were keeping their rooms. The cashier turns to the guest.) Very well, Mr. Foreman. You may sign the check with this pen.

請等一下。（出納員打電話問櫃檯，福門先生是否已登記，櫃檯員回答說：福門先生住在1502號套房，他們到海濱渡假一兩天，保留房間。出納員轉向這位客人）很好，福門先生。請你用這支筆簽名吧！

Walk-in guest

I can't write very well with my left hand. I had an accident and hurt my right hand. I couldn't tie my necktie, you see. (The cashier's telephone rings.)

我用左手寫得不好，我的右手意外受傷了，妳看，我連領帶都無法繫緊。（出納員的電話鈴響了。）

Cashier

Yes... Yes... Yes... Thank you. Now, Mr. Foreman, how do you want the money—in bills, small currency, or both? This check is for a hundred dollars. The service fee is one dollar.

是的…是的…是的，謝謝。福門先生，您要換成——紙幣、銅板，或者是兩種都要？這張支票面額是一百元，手續費一元。

Walk-in guest

I'd like the money in... (Just then the security takes hold of his arm.)

我想要的錢是……（就在這時，警衛人員捉住了他的手臂）。

Security

Let's go quietly, mister.

先生，我們靜靜地走吧！

Walk-in guest

What's wrong? I only want to cash my traveler's check.

什麼事啊？我只是想兌換我的旅行支票而已。

Security

Your check! Mr. Foreman called and reported that he lost his book of traveler's checks from the

National Trust Bank of Los Angeles.
你的支票！福門先生已經打電話報告，他的洛杉磯國際信託銀行的支票本遺失了。

Walk-in guest
That's impossible!
那是不可能的！

Security
You weren't fast enough. Mr. Foreman bought a newspaper just before he and his family got into the taxi. When he took out his wallet to pay the taxi driver, he saw that his book of checks was not there. So he called the hotel. He dropped his check book in front of the hotel when he bought the paper.
你的動作太慢了！福門先生在上計程車前買了報紙，當他下車要付車錢時，才發覺他的支票本遺失了。於是他打電話給旅館，他的支票本是在旅館前面，買報紙時掉的。

Walk-in guest
Didn't he go to the airport?
他不是到機場了嗎？

Security
How did you know he was going to the airport?
你怎麼知道他要去機場呢？

Walk-in guest
He told the cab driver. I heard him.
我聽到他告訴計程車司機的。

Security
Let's go quietly, mister. And take that bandage off your hand. Why did you try to forge a check?
先生，我們靜靜地走吧！把手上的繃帶拿掉。你為什麼要試著仿冒別人的簽名呢？

- walk-in　走進來；沒有訂房。

- front cashier　櫃檯收銀員、出納員。

- walk-in guest　沒有訂房直接進旅館的客人。

- cash　現金；兌現。

- traveler's check　旅行支票。

- local currency　當地的錢幣。

- rate of exchange　兌換率。

- cashier　收銀員。

- service charge　服務費、手續費。

- identification　身份證明。

- search　搜尋、找。

- suit　西裝。

- first check　第一張支票。

- book　本（支票）。

- occupies　佔用。

- beach　海邊。

- couple of days　二、三天；幾天。

- keeping their room　保留他們的房間。

- very well　很好。

- with this pen　用這支筆。

- tie　綁（領帶）。

- accident　意外事故。

- necktie　領帶。

- bill　鈔票、紙幣。

- small currency　銅板。
- what's wrong　怎麼了。
- lost　遺失。
- National Trust Bank　國際信託銀行。
- That's impossible!　那是不可能的。
- cab/taxi　計程車。
- bought　買。
- wallet　男用皮夾。

front cashier　櫃檯出納員

2. Baby sitter 保母 🔊 1-2-2

Miss Chen
Mr. Chang, this is Miss Chen, the relief maid. Tonight I am staying with the children in 1502. I'm sorry to disturb you, but...
張先生，我是輪班的保母陳小姐，今晚在1502號房照顧孩子，對不起打擾您，但是……。

Mr. Chang
What's the trouble, Miss Chen?
有什麼麻煩嗎，陳小姐？

Miss Chen
You see, sir, there are three children. Their mother told them to go to bed at 9:30. Well, first, they wanted to watch TV, but the set was broken.
先生，是這樣的，這三個孩子的媽媽告訴我，要他們九點半上床。不過，他們要看電視，可是電視機壞了。

Mr. Chang
Didn't you call the repairman to fix it?
你叫修理工人了嗎？

Miss Chen
Yes, he came and fixed it. But now the toilet in the boy's room won't work. There is water all over the bathroom floor.
是的，工人來修好了。可是現在男孩的浴室裡馬桶不通，所以浴室裡滿地都是水。

Mr. Chang
I'll send the plumber up right away, Miss Chen.
我會叫水管工人立即上來修理，陳小姐。

Miss Chen
Thank you. But the children also called room service and ordered a lot to eat.
謝謝。但是孩子們還叫了很多餐點到房裡吃。

Mr. Chang
Perhaps I had better come up.
(Soon Mr. Chang knocks at the door.)

或許我上來看看比較好。（很快的，張先生敲門。）

Miss Chen

(Shouting) Wait a minute. The door is locked, and I can't open it. (To Allen) I know you are behind those drapes, Allen. Come out and unlock the door. (Allen unlocks the door and Mr. Chang enters.)

（大聲地叫）等一下，門鎖住了，我打不開。（面對愛倫）我知道你在布簾後面，愛倫，出來把門打開。（愛倫把門打開，讓張先生進來。）

Mr. Chang

Isn't it time for little girls and boys to be in bed?
孩子們，你們上床的時間不是到了嗎？

Allen

I'm not little. Besides, we're hungry.
我不是小孩。而且我們都餓了。

Danny

He'll have his twelfth birthday next week. Mister, we always eat before we go to bed. (Just then the waiter brings in a tray with food and drinks. He puts the tray on the writing desk.)

先生，下星期是他十二歲的生日。我們經常在睡前要吃東西。（就在這時，服務員端著一大盤的餐點和飲料放在寫字檯上。）

Mr. Chang

Who is going to pay for all this?
這些帳誰來付啊？

Nancy

Allen will sign the bill.
愛倫會簽帳單。

Mr. Chang

What is your father going to say? Waiter, I had better O.K. this bill.
你爸會怎麼說的？服務員，我還是證明一下比較好。

Miss Chen

(Shaking her head) Your father won't like that.
（搖搖她的頭）你爸爸不會喜歡的。

Nancy Please put the tray on the coffee table in front of the sofa. We can eat while we are watching the programs.
請你把托盤放在沙發前面的咖啡桌上，我們可以邊吃邊看節目。

Mr. Chang Let's see if everything is here. What's on the tray?
叫的東西都來了嗎？讓我看看，托盤上有什麼東西？

Allen I ordered hamburgers, malted milk, and pie a la mode. I eat that every night.
我叫了漢堡（牛肉餅）、麥精牛奶和冰淇淋派。這些都是我每天晚上要吃的。

Danny And I do, too.
我也一樣。

Nancy I ordered a hot dog and cake. I like hot dog.
我叫了一份熱狗和蛋糕，我喜歡吃熱狗。

Miss Chen Of course, I'm going to tell their parents.
當然，我會告訴他們的爸媽。

Danny Miss, you're so nice. You aren't going to tell Daddy, are you? Here, you can have my ice cream.
小姐，妳太好了，妳不會告訴我爸的，對嗎？
來，我請妳吃冰淇淋。

- baby sitter　照顧小孩子的保母。
- maid　女傭。
- disturb　打擾。
- trouble　麻煩、煩惱。
- got to bed　上床。
- set　組、套。
- broken　被打破的。
- repair man　修護員。
- fix　修理。
- toilet　馬桶。廣意指「廁所」、「盥洗室」。
- won't work　壞了、不能用。
- all over　遍地。
- plumber　水管工人。
- room service　把餐點送到客房的服務。
- ordered　叫了、點了要吃的食物。
- knock　敲門。
- shout　叫、喊。
- drape　布縵。
- unlock　（打開）沒有上鎖。
- enter　進入。
- birthday　生日。
- waiter　餐廳的男服務員。
- tray　托盤。
- writing desk　寫字檯。

- bill　帳單。
- shake　搖動。
- coffee table　茶几。
- while　期間、當…期間。
- program　節目。
- hamburger　牛肉餅、漢堡。
- malted milk　麥精牛奶。
- pie a la mode　冰淇淋派。
- And so do I.　我也一樣。
- And I do, too.　我也是。
- hot dog　熱狗。
- cake　蛋糕。
- parents　父母親、雙親。
- Daddy　父親的暱稱。
- ice cream　冰淇淋。

Miss Chen

And now, Mr. Chang, come into the boys' bathroom, please. The water in the toilet is running over. (They enter the boys' bathroom. Miss Chen turns on the switch.) Look at the floor. It's like a swimming pool. Can you send someone to fix it?

張先生，請你到男孩的浴室，馬桶的水一直流個不停。（他們到浴室，陳小姐把關關打開）你看看，地面像是游泳池，請你叫人來修理好嗎？

Mr. Chang

Oh my goodness! What a lot of water! I'll call the maintenance department, and I'll also make a report to the housekeeper.

哦！我的天！這麼多的水，我立即通知養護部門和房務管理員。

Danny

What's a housekeeper?

什麼是房務管理員？

Mr. Chang

She's a very important person. She sees that everything is in good order. (Miss Chen returns to the living room, and Danny quietly walks into the bathroom.)

她是旅館的重要人員，她會使一切設備都正常。（陳小姐回到客廳，丹尼偷偷地走入浴室。）

Danny

Mister, I want to tell you something. Will you keep a secret?

先生，我要告訴你一些事情，請你要保守秘密，可以嗎？

Mr. Chang

Well, what is it?

好的，什麼事啊？

Danny

It was like this, mister. I was brushing my teeth, and I put my little red ball on the washbowl. Allen was in the shower. He opened the shower curtain and threw water on me. I threw the ball at him, but I slipped on the bath mat.

先生，事情是這樣的，我在刷牙的時候，把這個小紅球放在臉盆上，愛倫在沖水洗澡，他打開浴簾用水潑我，我拿球丟他，結果我滑倒在浴墊上。

Mr. Chang

Oh my goodness! Did you hurt yourself?

哦！我的天！你受傷了沒有？

Danny

Not much. I hit the bathtub, but the ball fell into the toilet bowl.

一點點。我碰到浴缸，可是球卻掉進馬桶裡。

Mr. Chang

Oh! So that's the trouble. Well, you are an honest lad. Don't worry. I believe the plumber can get the ball out. How old are you?

哦！原來是這樣啊！你是個誠實的孩子，不要擔心。我相信工人會把球拿出來的，你幾歲了？

Danny

I'm six years old. My name is Danny. Nancy is older than I am, and Allen is older than Nancy. He's the oldest, and he's the smartest.

我今年六歲，我叫丹尼，南西比我大，愛倫又比南西大，他（指愛倫）年紀最大，也是最聰明的。

Mr. Chang

You're smart, too. I have a niece whose name is Dolores. She is as old as you. She's six, too.

你也很聰明。我有一位姪女，叫得樂斯，她的年紀和你一樣，也是六歲。

Danny

Please, mister, don't tell that lady in there about the ball.

先生，請你不要把這件事，告訴那位小姐。

Mr. Chang Miss Chen is a good lady.
陳小姐是位好小姐。

Danny She's O.K. She's better than a lot of sitters. The best ones are the young ones.
她是很好，她比其他許多保母都要好，年輕的最好。

Mr. Chang Well, Danny, I used to be a boy myself. I won't tell anyone.
好吧！丹尼，我也是過來人，我不會告訴任何人的。

Danny Gee, thanks. You're a good guy. Here, take my hamburger.
咕，謝謝。你是大好人，我的漢堡請你吃。

Mr. Chang Thanks, but I'm not hungry now. I have to go. Good night, Danny.
謝謝，我還不餓，我要走了。晚安，丹尼。

Danny Good night, mister. So long.
晚安，先生。再見。

bathroom　浴室

- housekeeper　管理房間的主管人員。

- bathroom　浴室。

- switch　開關。

- Oh my goodness!　我的天啊！（感嘆語）。

- very important person　很重要的人（簡寫VIP）。

- good order　正常、井然有序。

- secret　秘密。

- brush　刷洗。

- washbowl　洗臉盆。

- in the shower　在沖浴。

- shower curtain　浴簾。

- threw water　潑水。

- slipped　滑倒。

- bath mat　浴墊。

- hurt　受傷。

- bathtub　浴缸。

- toilet bowl　馬桶。

- honest lad　老實的少年。

- older　年紀較大。

- oldest　年紀最大。

- smartest　最聰明。

- niece　姪女。

- better than　好於、更好於。

- guy　男人，口頭語、與fellow相同。

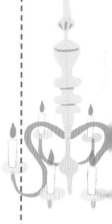

Assistant manager

It is my pleasure, Miss Susan Sarandon, to welcome you to our hotel. We hope that your stay will be a pleasant one.

這是我的榮幸，蘇珊‧夏蘭敦小姐，歡迎妳光臨本飯店。我們希望妳住在這兒會有愉快的時光。

Miss Sarandon

And who are you, young man?

你是誰呀！年輕人？

Assistant manager

I am Scott Kao, the assistant manager, at your service.

我是高副理，將為妳效勞。

Miss Sarandon

And where is the manager?

經理不在是嗎？

Assistant manager

Mr. Pan, the manager sends his regrets. He is out of town, attending a convention. If there is anything you want, please call me. I'd be honored to help the most beautiful actress in the world, Susan Sarandon.

經理潘先生要我代為致歉。他離開這裡參加一項會議。如果妳有什麼吩咐，請告訴我。我非常榮幸能為世界上最美麗的明星，蘇珊‧夏蘭敦小姐服務。

Miss Sarandon

You know that I came here for a rest and do not want to be disturbed. Miss Harris, my secretary, will take all messages. (Turning to Miss Harris.) What about those reporters and photographers at the airport? They're coming here, aren't they?

你知道我是來這裡休憩的，我不希望有任何打擾。哈利斯小姐是我的秘書，她會處理所有的留言。（面對哈利斯小姐）那些在機場的記者及攝影記者怎麼樣了？他們會不會跟來這裡，會嗎？

Miss Harris

I told them to come here at half past four. You will be more rested then.
我告訴他們四點半來。妳可以充份地休息。

Assistant manager

Miss Sarandon, are those your dogs?
夏蘭敦小姐，這些都是妳的狗嗎？

Miss Sarandon

These are my darlings.
這些是我的寶貝。

Assistant manager

I'm very sorry, but it is against regulations of the hotel to allow dogs in the rooms. Mr. Pan is very strict about that, because many people are allergic to dogs.
非常抱歉，飯店規定不可以帶狗進房間裡，潘經理管得很嚴，因為有很多人對狗會敏感。

Miss Sarandon

But I have the Royal Suite. Surely my pets can come there with me, can't they? Besides, who is allergic to dogs?
我住皇家套房。我應該可以和我的寵物在一起的，不行嗎？是誰對狗會敏感？

Assistant manager

Don't you think they will be happier in a special room we have for them down here?
妳是否可以考慮，讓牠們住在特別設置的房間裡，牠們會覺得更愉快哦？

Miss Sarandon

Barbara, see about the babies' accommodation, and give the chef their special menus.
芭芭拉，看看寶貝房，交給大廚，牠們（狗的）的特別菜單。

Miss Sarandon

Achoo! I must speak to Mr ... Achoo! To Mr. Kao.
哈啾！我一定要和……先生講話，哈啾！找高先生。

Telephone operator

Mr. Kao? Wait a moment please. (A few minutes later.) I'm sorry, Mr. Kao has left.

高先生嗎？請等一下。（幾分鐘後）對不起，高先生剛剛走開。

Miss Sarandon

Left the hotel? Achoo! Achoo! Call him back! Hundreds of roses are in all the rooms. I'm allergic to roses. Achoo! My eyes! My nose! Oh! And the photographers are coming this afternoon!

他離開飯店了嗎？哈啾！哈啾！叫他回來！一大堆玫瑰花放在我的房間。我對玫瑰花會過敏。哈啾！我的眼睛！我的鼻子！哦！攝影記者今天下午就要來了！

- welcome you to our hotel　歡迎光臨本飯店。

- young man　年輕人。

- at your service　隨時爲您效勞。

- regret　抱歉的、遺憾的。

- attend　參加、出席。

- actress　女演員。

- for a rest　要休息。

- reporter　採訪記者。

- photographer　攝影記者。

- darling　親愛的。

- against　違反。

- regulation　規定。

- strict　嚴格的。

- allergic　敏感、過敏症（醫學的）。

- Royal Suite　帝王套房。

- pet(s)　寵物（貓狗等）。

- chef　廚師。

- special menu　特別食譜。

- left　左（邊）；離開；留下。

- actor　男演員。

Mr. Winner
Good afternoon, Miss Wang. I'm Peter Winner. Here's my card. I was sent by Asia Travel Magazine to write a story about hotels in this chain.
午安，王小姐。我的名字叫做彼得‧溫拿，這是我的名片。我是亞洲旅遊雜誌派來的，要寫一篇關於你們旅館連鎖經營的報導。

P. R. director
How do you do, Mr. Winner? Of course we always like favorable publicity. Why did you choose our hotels?
你好嗎？溫拿先生。我們當然喜歡有更好的宣傳。你為什麼要選我們的旅館呢？

Mr. Winner
Your chain has a very good reputation, you know.
你們的連鎖經營系統有非常好的名譽，你是知道的。

P. R. director
That's true. What ideas do you have in mind?
那是事實。你心中有什麼好的主意嗎？

Mr. Winner
I want to tell things as they are and show why your hotel attracts more tourists. Is it because of your hospitality, service, comforts, entertainments, cuisine or what? Will you take me around?
我要忠實地報導為什麼你們的旅館，能夠吸引這麼多的觀光客。是因為你們旅館的招待、服務、舒適、節目、烹飪或其他什麼原因？請妳帶我參觀一下好嗎？

P. R. director
With pleasure.
非常樂意。

Mr. Winner
I'm so glad that you speak English. You speak it very well.
很高興妳會說英語。妳說得非常好。

P. R. director Thank you. English lessons are given to all our employees, that is, if they want to learn the language.
謝謝你。我們所有員工都有英語課程，也就是說，假使他們願意學習的話。

Mr. Winner What a good idea. I'll include that in my story. Americans and English people will feel comfortable here. Are you going to be busy later this afternoon?
真是一個好主意。我也要將這個報導在內。美國人和英國人住在這裡會感到很舒服。今天下午你會很忙嗎？

P. R. director Look at my schedule. In twenty minutes I have to listen a new group of entertainers from London. They are called the "Chimpanzees". They perform in our night club, the Pink Cat. Haven't you heard them?
看看我的時間表。20分鐘之內，我要接待一個由倫敦來的藝人團體。他們叫做「非洲黑猩猩」。在本飯店的「粉紅貓」夜總會表演，你聽說過沒有？

Mr. Winner No, I haven't heard them myself. But I have read that they are very good.
沒有，我還沒聽過。但我讀過有關他們的報導，相當好。

P. R. director Then at two o'clock there is a luncheon for advertising executives. Pictures must be taken. After that at four o'clock there is a tea and fashion show given for charity. I must arrange photographs of the society ladies and of the models.
然後二點鐘，有廣告業經理的午宴。拍照過後，四點有一個慈善的時裝表演茶會。我要安排名流仕女們及模特兒的拍照。

Mr. Winner Couldn't I help you on that exciting assignment?
可不可以讓我幫妳做這種多彩多姿的差事？

P. R. director I'd certainly like some help. I'll be here until nine o'clock. We have a lot of conventions, conferences, banquets, and meetings here.
我當然希望有幫手。我會待在這裡到九點，我們有許多的集會、會議、宴會、座談會在這裡舉行。

Mr. Winner That's what brings in the profits. When can we meet tomorrow?
這才是賺鈔票之道。明天什麼時候再見面？

P. R. director How about eight-thirty? I have less work in the morning.
八點三十分怎麼樣？早上我的工作較少。

Mr. Winner Fine. What about having a cocktail this evening when you have finished? We could begin our work in the bar. You can tell me what the ladies said.
很好。妳今晚工作完後，我們來杯雞尾酒如何？我們可以在酒吧開始工作。妳可以告訴我那些仕女們說些什麼？

P. R. director Thank you, but my fiancé is calling for me at nine o'clock.
謝謝，可是我的未婚夫今晚九點要打電話給我。

Mr. Winner Is that being hospitable to a lonely guest?
這是待客之道嗎？

088

- public relations desk　公共關係櫃檯。
- P. R. director　公共關係經理。
- Asia Travel Magazine　亞洲旅遊雜誌。
- chain (hotel)　連鎖（旅館）、連鎖經營。
- favorable　良好的、有利的。
- publicity　宣傳。
- reputation　名譽、名聲。
- in mind　心裡、心中。
- attract　吸引。
- tourist　觀光客。
- hospitality　對待客人很親切、週到的服務。
- service　服務。
- comforts　舒適、舒服。
- entertainment　娛樂活動；宴會；招待。
- cuisine　烹飪、料理。
- take me around　帶我走一趟；看一看。
- employee　員工。
- language　語言。
- schedule　進度表。
- entertainer　宴會的接待者；表演的藝人。
- London　倫敦。
- Chimpanzee　非洲特有的一種黑猩猩。
- perform　表演。
- Pink Cat　粉紅貓。

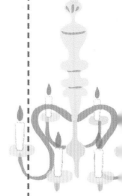

- luncheon　午宴。
- advertising　廣告。
- executive　主管、代表。
- fashion show　時裝表演。
- charity　慈善。
- society ladies　社交界的仕女們。
- exciting　很興奮的；很有趣的。
- assignment　安排。
- lonely　寂寞的、孤獨的。
- banquet　宴會。

Mr. Thomson (Looking at a calling card.) Good afternoon, Miss Lo. I see that you represent the Meriden Hotel. What brings you hear?

（正在看名片）午安，羅小姐，你是美麗殿大飯店的代表，有何貴幹嗎？

Miss. Lo We have been informed that your company is holding its international sales convention here next spring. I came to offer you the services of our hotel.

我們已經知道，貴公司明年春天，將舉行國際業務會議。我是來向您說明，我們飯店所提供的服務。

Mr. Thomson How did you find that out? I was notified only this week, myself.

你怎麼知道的？這個星期我才知道的。

Miss. Lo It's our business to give you quick service, Mr. Thomson. I know you are well acquainted with our facilities, as you have attended many banquets, dinners and luncheons there. You know that we are prepared to accommodate large crowds, and you know that we have more advantages to offer your people than any other hotel. Our French chef has the finest reputation in town, and our banquet manager is very efficient. Our hotel is well known for its service and courtesy.

提供您快捷的服務是我們的責任，湯姆生先生，您曾經參加過很多次我們飯店的宴會，晚餐及午餐，所以很了解我們的設施，我們是專為大型會議而設計的，比起其他飯店，我們有更多的便利提供給您。我們的法國主廚在這個城市裡，是最負聲譽的，宴會經理辦

事效率非常高。我們的飯店被公認是服務和禮貌最好的。

Mr. Thomson
Yes, I have often been entertained at your very fine hotel.
是的，我經常在你們的飯店應酬。

Miss. Lo
Have you been in any of the rooms？The rooms in our hotel are all outside rooms with lovely views. They are beautifully decorated and comfortable. Here are some pictures. Your people will enjoy not only the luxuries of our hotel, but also the location as well. It's in the heart of the City, near the shopping district, north of a main boulevard, not far from a beautiful park.
您住過我們的客房嗎？我們的客房全部面向外，風景很美。裝潢高貴而舒適。這裡有幾張照片。您的客人將享受豪華的設備和便利的位置。在市中心地區，靠近商店，大馬路的北方，離那美麗的公園也不遠。

Mr. Thomson
Yes, I know all that is true, but your prices are high.
是的，我知道那是真的，不過，你們的價錢也不便宜。

Miss. Lo
Mr. Thomson, for large conventions we can meet the price of any other hotel in the city. We give you that assurance. Besides, we'll arrange a special hospitality room for your group here with our compliments.
湯姆生先生，這麼大的會議，我們的價錢不會比人家的貴。我們可以給您保證。而且我們將安排一間特別的接待室給您的團體使用，這是我們的一番心意（免費的）。

Mr. Thomson
Well, young man, arranging conventions is out of my line. I'm just the president of the company. I'll leave that job to Mr. Resor, the vice president in charge of sales. Just a minute. (Mr. Thomson presses a button on the intercom system.) Mr. Resor, can you see Miss Lo. of the Meriden Hotel right now? ... Good. I'll send him down. Miss Lo, Mr. Resor will be glad to talk over details with you. If your price is right, you have my approval.

好吧！年輕人，會議的安排並不是我管的。我只是公司的董事長而已。我想這份工作讓主管業務的副董事長黎索先生來決定。請等一下。（湯姆生先生按對講機）黎索先生，現在你可以接見美麗殿大飯店的羅小姐嗎？好的，我叫他下來。羅小姐，黎索先生很高興和你談談細節的事情。如果你的價錢合理，我會同意的。

meeting room　小型會議室

- calling card　名片。
- represent　表示；代表。
- informed　已通知。
- international sales convention　國際業務會議。
- notified　已告知。
- quick service　快速服務。
- be acquainted with　熟悉。
- facilities　設施。
- advantage　利益的；便利。
- banquet manager　宴會經理。
- efficient　效率。
- outside room　向外房。
- location　位置。
- luxuries　奢侈品。
- heart of the city　市中心。
- shopping district　購物區。
- main boulevard　林蔭大道。
- park　公園。
- assurance　保證；自信。
- hospitality room　接待套房。
- compliments　致贈。
- out of my line　不是我的業務範圍。
- in charge of　負責，主持。
- intercom system　對講機系統。

- send him down 　叫他下來。
- talk over 　商談一下。
- detail 　細節。
- approval 　同意、認可。

1. 國際旅館類型區分

為方便旅客選擇住宿旅館，國際上通常將旅館作以下的區分：

1. 商業旅館（COMMERCIAL HOTEL）：以商務旅客為主，最基本的服務應有：免費供應晨報及早上咖啡（MORNING COFFEE）、專人行李服務、差遣服務、接待及諮詢服務，客房餐飲服務、洗衣服務、醫療服務、訂房及訂票（位）服務，設施應有：商務中心、客房上網及舒適備品、正式餐廳、咖啡廳、酒廊、宴會及會議廳、洗衣房、商店街、俱樂部、健身房、游泳池、三溫暖、空調系統及安全系統等。

2. 機場旅館（AIRPORR HOTEL）：以搭機、轉機及過境旅客為主。機場旅館之服務與設施和商業旅館差異不大。

3. 經濟旅館（ECONOMY HOTEL）：以較低消費旅客為主。僅提供清潔的房間及簡單的服務，旅館設備也較有限。

4. 套房旅館（SUITE HOTEL）：以中短期住用為主。一或

二間，附浴室及客廳，設小廚房、小吧檯及冰箱。

5. 公寓旅館（APARTMENT/RESIDENTIAL HOTEL）：以長期住用爲主。提供房務管理服務及房間餐飲服務。通常設有餐廳。

6. 賭場旅館（CASINO HOTEL）：大型休閒旅館。旅館內設置各種賭博設施，大型餐廳、酒廊、夜總會及秀場等。

7. 度假旅縮（RESORT HOTEL）：以度假住宿爲主。現代高級度假旅館，其服務與設施和商業旅館相同。度假旅館依其性質不同，約可區分爲：

　　・夏季度假旅館（SUMMER RESORT）
　　・冬季度假旅館（WINTER RESORT）
　　・山區度假旅館（MOUNTAIN RESORT）
　　・海濱度假旅館（BEACH RESORT）
　　・水療度假旅館（SPA & HEALTH RESORT）
　　・住宅度假旅館（CONDO－RESORT）

② 旅館等級的標示

國際旅館等級評鑑

世界觀光組織（WORLD TOURISM ORGANIZATION簡稱「WTO」）訂立「旅館等級基本標準」，由「一星」至「五星」均有詳細標準説明，並以「★」號標示等級：

　　★　　　AVERAGE COMFORT
　　★★　　GOOD COMFORT
　　★★★　GREAT COMFORT
　　★★★★　VERY GREAT COMFORT
　★★★★★ GREAT LUXURY

英國：

旅館等級評鑑，由：

◎英國旅遊局　以皇冠標示。

◎英國汽車協會　以「★」標示一至五星。

　一星　小規模但設施及裝潢良好，提供餐飲服務。

　二星　比一星級旅館要好。

　三星　規模較大，設施較多，更好的餐飲服務。

　四星　高標準設施及服務，最舒適的住宿。

　五星　除四星標準外，更具豪華，達到國際認定標準。

◎皇家汽車會　以「★」標示一至五星。

日本：

對於旅館沒有等級評鑑，依日本「旅館業法」將日本的旅
館區分為四種：

◎HOTEL（ホテル）

◎旅館

◎簡易宿泊

◎下宿

美國：

旅館等級評鑑，由AAA「美國汽車協會」及「美孚石油公
司」執行，旅館自由參加，不收任何費用。

◎AAA以鑽石「◆」標示。

　　◆　住宿達到普通標準，房間符合清潔及舒適。
　　　這個等級的基本標準是：舒適（Comfort）、
　　　隱私（Privacy）、清潔（Cleanliness）、安全
　　　（Safety）。

　　◆◆　除具備◆一顆鑽石的標準外，更提升旅館的裝潢及
　　　傢俱的品質。這個等級的旅館，不管是新建的或
　　　古老的，均提供較多的餐館服務，適合經濟級的
　　　旅客住用。

　　◆◆◆　提供更高服務標準，日常用品種類增加，服務及
　　　設備也較好，強調服務品質及舒適感。

　　◆◆◆◆　表示高標準的優良旅館，服務專業化，設備多樣
　　　化，用品高質感。

◆◆◆◆◆列為最佳的著名旅館，提供非常專業而高貴的服務。設備豪華，用品高貴而多量，提供完整無瑕疵的設備，服務表現專業而富技巧，令人感受愉快。

◎美孚以「★」標示：

★ 良好，水準以上（good, better than average）

★★ 很好（very good）

★★★ 非常好（excellent）

★★★★ 傑出的（outstanding-worth a special trip）

★★★★★ 國家最好之一（one of the best in the country）

Chapter 2 RESTAURANT 餐廳

一、接待業務

1. The breakfast 早餐 🔊2-1-1

Captain
(Greeting Mr. Foreman, Allen-a young teenager, Nancy—about ten, and Danny—about six) Good morning. A table for four? Follow me, please, over here.
（打招呼對著福門先生、愛倫十幾歲、南西約十歲、丹尼約六歲）早安，四位嗎？請跟我來，在這邊。

Danny
Mommy didn't come with us. She's going to eat breakfast in bed.
媽媽沒跟我們一道來，她在房內用早餐。

Nancy
May we sit near the window? I like to watch people in the streets.
我們靠窗邊坐好嗎？我喜歡看街上走來走去的人。

Captain
Of course. There's an empty booth over there.
當然可以，那邊有一個空位子。

Waitress
(Smiling, handing them menus) Would you like to look at the menu?
（微笑著，給他們菜單）您要看看菜單嗎？

Mr. Foreman
I don't need one. I always order the same—ham, two fried eggs, easy over, a stack of wheat cakes and coffee. We'll begin with a large glass of orange juice.
不必了，我都叫一樣的：火腿、二個煎蛋雙面煎、一些烤餅和咖啡，先給我們大杯的柳橙汁。

(100)

Nancy
Well, I don't want oatmeal. We usually eat those at home. We're trying to win a prize. If we save fifty coupons we can get a plastic air-chair.
我不要麥糊，我們在家常常吃，是想要得獎，如果我們積

存50張券，就可以得到一張塑膠的空氣坐墊。

Waitress An air-chair? What's that?
空氣坐墊？那是什麼呀？

Nancy It's a round chair. You blow it up with air. It'll be great for TV or the beach. Wait a minute. I want something different for breakfast.
那是個圓墊子，吹進空氣它會脹大起來，看電視或到海邊時很好用。等一下，我要一些和家裡不一樣的早餐。

Danny Allen, what's this "Continental breakfast"?
愛倫，什麼叫做「歐陸早餐」？

Allen It's a continental breakfast, Danny—rolls, juice, and coffee.
丹尼，歐陸早餐，就是麵包捲、果汁和咖啡。

Mr. Foreman You want more than that, son. Why don't you order a nice....?
你要多點一些，孩子，為什麼不點好一點的呢…？

Danny Look! Is that watermelon over there? That's what I want—watermelon. I like that every day.
你看！那邊不是西瓜嗎？西瓜，那就是我想要的，我每天都很愛吃。

Waitress Yes, watermelons are very good. Don't you want anything else—waffles with syrup or honey?
是的，西瓜很好，你還要不要其他的：華富餅加甜漿或蜂蜜？

Danny What's a waffle？
什麼是華富餅？

Nancy You know, Danny. We have them at home. They're in squares.

丹尼，你知道的，我們在家吃過，四方型的。

Waitress They're like pancakes, only not fried.
像是薄餅，只是不用煎的。

Danny Yes, waffles. You know everything I like, don't you?
好的，華富餅。你知道我所要的東西，不是嗎？

Allen I'm going to have French toast, sausages, and hot chocolate.
我要法國土司、香腸和熱巧克力。

Nancy Mushroom omelette, raisin muffins, and malted milk for me. I like malts.
我要洋菇歐姆蛋、葡萄乾麵包、麥芽牛奶。我喜歡麥芽。

Danny So do I, please. (Mary repeats the orders. Soon Tony brings the tray of food, Mary serves the food to the guests.)
我也一樣（瑪莉重念了一遍他們所點的菜，很快的湯尼把餐送上來，瑪莉一一送到客人面前）。

Allen Is this French toast? It doesn't look like French toast.
這是法國土司嗎？看起來不像是法國土司。

Waitress Oh, no. It's cinnamon toast. There's a mistake. I'm sorry. I'll change it.
哦，這是肉桂土司，弄錯了，對不起，我給你換過來。

Allen Oh, no. Don't change it. It looks good.
不必換了，看起來還不錯。

Nancy My hot chocolate is cold.
我的熱巧克力涼了。

Waitress (Looking at her order book) Don't you want malted milk?
（看她的點菜本子）妳不是要麥芽牛奶的嗎？

102

Nancy

Oh, yes, of course. I'm sorry.
哦，對了，很抱歉。

Mr. Foreman

This cup isn't clean. This looks like lipstick on the rim.
這個杯子不乾淨，好像有口紅在杯緣上。

Waitress

I'll get a clean cup right away. (At that moment Tony passes. He is carrying a tray full of dishes.)
我立刻給您換個乾淨的。（正在這時湯尼經過，他端著滿托盤的盤子。）

Danny

(Jumping up quickly) Look! A parade! (Danny's head hits Tony's tray. Tony grabs the tray with both hands, but a few glasses fall. One glass breaks.)
（很快的跳起來）看！遊行！（丹尼的頭碰到了湯尼的托盤，湯尼二隻手握住托盤，幾個杯子掉下，一個破了。）

Mr. Foreman

Son, don't get excited. You must always look before you leap. Danny. It's all right. (The Captain comes to the Foremans' table. She talks to Tony).
孩子，不要太興奮，跳的時候一定要先注意，湯尼，沒什麼關係。（領班走過來福門這桌，他跟湯尼說話。）

Mr. Foreman

Please don't blame the busboy. It wasn't his fault. My son hit the tray. I'll pay for the damage.
請妳不要責怪見習生，不是他的過失，而是我的孩子碰到了托盤，這些損失由我負責好了。

Captain

It's all right, sir. Don't worry. Sit down and enjoy your breakfast.
不要緊的，先生，請坐下享用您的早餐。

- breakfast　早餐。

- captain　領班。

- a table for four?　四位一桌嗎？

- over here　在這裡。

- over there　在那邊。

- eat breakfast in bed　在房間裡用早餐（在床上）。

- near the window　靠窗戶邊的。

- in the street　在街道上。

- empty booth　空的位子。booth是指二個沙發相對，中間有桌子的位子。

- ham　火腿。

- fried egg　煎蛋。

- easy over　雙面煎。

- stack　一堆。

- wheat cake　（hot cake）烤餅。

- usually　平常、一般。

- prize　獎品。

- coupon　券（meal coupon餐券）。

- plastic　塑膠。

- air-chair　空氣坐墊。

- blow it up　吹起來。

- different　不同的、不一樣的。

- continental breakfast　歐陸式早餐。

- watermelon　西瓜。

- waffle　華富餅。

- round chair　圓的墊子（坐墊）。
- syrup　甜漿。
- honey　蜂蜜。
- square　四方型的。
- pancake　薄餅（用煎的）。
- French toast　法國土司。
- sausage　香腸。
- mushroom omelette　洋菇歐姆蛋（蛋捲）。
- raisin muffins　葡萄乾麵包。
- malted milk　麥芽牛奶。
- repeats the order　所點的菜再重複說一遍。
- cinnamon toast　肉桂土司。
- I'll change it.　我會給您換過來。
- lipstick　口紅。
- on the rim　在（杯子的）邊緣。
- jump up　跳起來。
- parade　遊行。
- hit　碰到、打到。
- grab　捉住。
- fall　掉下來。
- break　破了。
- get excited　（太）興奮。
- leap　跳。
- blame　責怪、責備。
- fault　過失、過錯。
- damage　損失、損壞。
- enjoy your breakfast　享用您的早餐。

1. 早餐的蛋類

Fried egg	煎蛋
Boiled egg	煮蛋（帶殼）
Poached egg	煮蛋（去殼）
Scrambled egg	炒蛋
Omelet	蛋捲、歐姆蛋

FRIED EGG

straight up
sunnysid up
單面煎，蛋黃半生熟

over easy　　　　　雙面煎，蛋黃半生熟

over hard　　　　　雙面煎，蛋黃全熟

BOILED EGG

soft boiled egg-three minutes	三分鐘，蛋白半熟
medium boiled egg-five minutes	五分鐘，蛋白全熟
hard boiled egg	蛋黃全熟

2. Luncheon for tourist 觀光客的午餐 🔊 2-1-2

Tour guide

Are the box lunches ready for the ladies going on my trip? They're eating breakfast now, aren't they? I gave the manager their orders yesterday.

給女士們遊覽用的午餐餐盒準備好了沒有？她們正在吃早餐是嗎？昨天我已將菜單交給經理了。

Captain

Everything is O.K. I just saw the box lunches in the kitchen. I checked the number and have the order here. The assistant chef does a good job with picnic lunches. He wrapped the sandwiches and cake in separate plastic bags. He made everything attractive and neat. People are fussy about cleanliness, you know.

全部都做好了。我剛才在廚房裡看到餐盒，我查過數量，沒錯，助理廚師把餐盒做得非常好，他把三明治和蛋糕分開裝入塑膠袋，他做事乾淨俐落，你知道的，客人對於清潔是很仔細的。

Tour guide

They were fussy about these orders, too. No one ordered the same thing. Everyone wanted something different.

(The captain asks the busboy to bring out the boxes.)

她們對這些菜單也是很挑剔的。沒有一位點的是相同的，每個人都點的不一樣。

（領班叫見習生把餐盒拿出來。）

Captain

Here they are. The cook wrote the contents on each box. There are two sandwiches in each box: ham and cheese, chicken salad, tuna fish, peanut butter and jelly, and roast beef with mustard.

這些就是，每盒廚師都寫上內容了，每盒二個三明治、火腿和起司、雞肉沙拉、鮪魚、花生醬和果醬，還有紅燒牛肉加芥末。

Tour guide What about the box for the lady on a special diet?
對於那位女士的特別餐盒呢？

Captain The head chef took charge of her lunch himself. He prepares all her meals according to her doctor's instructions. Her name is on the box.
主廚親自負責調製，都按照她的醫生所指示而準備，餐盒上有她的名字。

Tour guide Isn't there anything else besides sandwiches?
除了三明治外，還有些什麼呢？

Captain Of course, the usual—devilled eggs, pickles, two salads in plastic cups—cold slaw and fruit jello—a big red apple, an orange, and a slice of mocha cake.
當然有啊，一般是魔鬼蛋、泡菜、二盒的沙拉、生菜和水果果凍，一個大的紅蘋果、柳橙、一塊摩卡蛋糕。

Tour guide That sounds good. What about the drinks?
的確很好，飲料呢？

Captain The usual—assorted fruit juices, ginger ale, cola drinks, bottled water. Nobody wanted a thermos of hot drinks. Would you like beer for yourself?
有什錦果汁、薑汁飲料、可樂、蒸餾水，沒人要保溫飲料，您要啤酒嗎？

Tour guide No thanks. I never drink while I'm driving. Are the bottles in the cold container?
不要，謝謝，我開車從不喝酒。飲料是不是放在冰桶裡？

Captain Yes, everything's ready, and everybody's ready, too. I'll have the boys put the food in the bus. Your car's near the entrance, isn't it?

是的，東西都預備好了，每個人也準備好了，我叫服務員把餐盒搬入車裡，你的車子靠近門口，不是嗎？

Tour guide Yes, here's the key. (Batting his stomach) Oh, I ate too much. I won't want any lunch after that big breakfast steak and hash brown potatoes. May I have a toothpick?

鑰匙在這裡（拍著他的肚皮）哦！我吃太多了，一份牛排和煎馬鈴薯，午餐可以不用吃了，給我一支牙籤好嗎？

Captain (Passing a toothpick container) Take several. Goodbye and good luck. Have a good time!
(Mr. Foreman signals to the captain.)

（遞過牙籤罐）拿幾支吧，再見，祝您好運，玩得痛快！（福門先生做了手勢叫領班。）

Captain Yes, sir, what may I do for you?

是的，先生，您要什麼嗎？

Mr. Foreman The children are going to visit the zoo today. Could you fix a lunch for them to take along?

孩子們今天要去參觀動物園，請你做餐盒給他們帶去可以嗎？

Captain Yes, indeed, sir. What time will they be leaving?

當然可以，先生。什麼時候去啊？

Mr. Foreman In about an hour. They got up early this morning. They want to go sightseeing. The housekeeper recommended a very nice maid to go with them. The guide from the tourist agency here is taking them.

約一個小時後，今天他們起得早，要去觀光，房務管

理員推薦了一位很好的女傭陪他們一起去，旅行社的導遊安排他們去參觀。

Captain That's fine. We'll fix up a basket for five. What would they like?
很好，我準備好一籃五份，他們喜歡什麼？

Allen Can we have hamburgers?
我們可以要漢堡嗎？

Nancy And hot dogs and cake?
我還要熱狗和蛋糕。

Danny I like donuts.
我要甜甜圈。

Captain We'll prepare a lot of goodies for you—nice surprises in your basket. How about that?
我們會準備許多糖果，讓你在打開盒子時驚奇一下，這樣好嗎？

- Tour guide (escort)　導遊。
- picnic lunch　野餐盒。
- box lunch　（午餐）餐盒。
- trip　旅行、旅遊。
- everything　一切事情。
- kitchen　廚房。
- assistant chef　助理廚師（head chef主廚）。
- wrapped　包裝好的。
- sandwiches　三明治。
- cake　蛋糕。
- plastic bag　塑膠袋。
- attractive　吸引人的。
- fussy　仔細、小心。
- cleanliness　清潔、乾淨。
- content(s)　內容。
- cheese　起司。
- chicken salad　雞肉沙拉。
- tuna fish　鮪魚。
- peanut butter　花生醬。
- jelly　果醬。
- roast beef　烤牛排。
- mustard　芥末。
- special diet　特殊食品（如：減肥食品）。
- doctor's instruction　醫師指示的（說明的）。

- besides 作「除外」解。
- devilled egg 魔鬼蛋。
- pickle 泡菜。
- cold slaw 生菜。
- fruit jello 水果果凍。
- a slice 一片。
- mocha cake 摩卡蛋糕。
- ginger ale 薑汁飲料（不含酒精）。
- cola drinks 可樂。
- bottled water 蒸餾水。
- beer 啤酒。
- cold container 冰桶。
- entrance 入口。
- bus 巴士。
- hash brown potatoes 絞肉混合馬鈴薯一起煎。
- toothpick container 牙籤罐。
- good luck 祝你好運。
- Have a good time! 玩得痛快。
- zoo 動物園。
- sightseeing 觀光。
- tourist agency 旅行社。
- hamburger 漢堡（牛肉餅夾麵包）。
- hot dog 熱狗（醃肉腸夾麵包）。
- donuts 甜甜圈。
- goodies (goody) 糖果。
- surprise(s) 驚奇。

Waiter What would you like to order, please?
請問妳要點什麼菜？

Betty I don't know yet, but I don't care for the specials today. I don't like either croquette or ragout. I'm going to order à la carte.
我還沒想出來，不過我不要今天的特餐，也不喜歡吃炸肉餅和燉肉，我要點菜。

Lona Chicken croquettes? What are they?
是炸雞肉嗎？那是什麼菜？

Waiter They're...well, they are made out of chicken and potatoes, and they are...well, they look like a cone. I just saw them. They're very good.
那是…嗯，那是用雞肉和馬鈴薯做的，那是…嗯，那像是圓錐形的筒。我剛才還看到，很好吃。

Sally I don't like leftovers. What's this cheese soufflé like?
我不要吃剩菜，「起司舒芙蕾」是像什麼東西？
（soufflé是一種甜點。）

Waiter It's very good. It's cheese. Well...it's a soufflé。
那個不錯，是起司。嗯！那是「舒芙蕾（蛋切酥）」。

Sally How is it made? Is it melted over toast?
是什麼做的？是不是土司包麥精粉呢？

Waiter No, I don't think so. I'll find out.
不，我想不是，我去問問看。

Lona Is this ham mousse good?
這個火腿慕斯好不好？（mousse是一種甜品。）

Waiter Yes, it is.
不錯呀。

Sally Is it "mouse" or "moose", and how is it made?
是Mouse（鼠）還是Moose（麋），那是怎麼做的？

Waiter It's made with ham.
用火腿做的。

Sally Is the sautéed kidney cooked in the oven?
這道「嫩煎腰子」是否用烤箱烤的？

Waiter I don't think so. I'll ask the headwaiter.
我想不是的，我問問領班。

Betty I've made up my mind. I'd like hors d'oeuvres—pâté de foie gras. Is the paté made here, or is it canned?
我已經想好要吃的東西了，我要鵝肝醬，它是現做的，還是罐頭的？

Waiter We make our own pâté. It's very good.
是我們自己做的鵝肝醬，非常好吃。

Sally What are mushrooms au gratin?
烘洋菇是什麼？

Waiter They are very good mushrooms. I think they're served with a white sauce.
那是很好的洋菇，我想那是加白醬汁的。

Betty For dessert, I'll have fromage and crackers. Let me see what kind you serve.
甜點，我要奶酪和蘇打餅干。讓我看看你們有什麼？

Sally What is the bombe glacée!
什麼是「甜瓜冰淇淋」？

Waiter Wait a minute please. I'll have to ask the headwaiter. (Waiter hurries away, and the girls laugh.)
請等一下，我要問領班（服務員急匆匆地走開，小姐們笑了）。

Sally We really were very naughty to that nice young waiter. Here comes the headwaiter. We'd better be serious. I'm sure he knows his French.
(Waiter goes to another table. A man has just come in from the swimming pool. He has on bathing trunks and a bathrobe. He is barefooted.)
我們對那位年輕的服務員開夠玩笑了。領班來了，我們最好正經些，我想他是知道法文的。
（服務員換到另一張檯子，一位先生剛從游泳池進來，他只穿了游泳褲和浴袍，打赤腳。）

Waiter Excuse me, sir, but in the Royal Room, all men must wear pants and a shirt and jacket.
對不起，先生，來皇家西餐廳用餐的客人都要衣冠整齊的（穿著長褲、襯衫和外套）。

Guest What? What? Jackets?
什麼？什麼？衣冠整齊？

Waiter Yes, sir. That is the rule.
先生，是的，那是我們的規定。

Guest Bring me a menu. I'm hungry.
給我菜單，我餓了。

Waiter Well, sir. I have to obey orders. They told me not to serve a guest if he isn't properly dressed.
嗯，先生，我一定要服從上級的命令，我不能為衣著不整的人服務的。

Guest What's wrong with a bathrobe? I've got more clothes on than those girls.

穿浴衣有什麼不對的？我穿的比那些女孩子還多呢！

Waiter Just a minute, sir. (The headwaiter arrives.)
先生，請等一下（領班走過來）。

Headwaiter I'm sorry, sir. We can't serve you here. If you go to the pool, we'll send your lunch out there.
先生，對不起，我們不能在這裡為您服務。如果您到游泳池，我們會將您的午餐送到游泳池邊的。

Guest But I like to eat with people. I don't want to eat it in my room.
我喜歡在人多的地方用餐。我不想在我的房裡吃東西。

Headwaiter I must insist, sir. Please don't make me call the detective. If you put on a pair of pants, a shirt and a jacket, we'll be pleased to serve you here.
先生，我不能改變。請不要因此而麻煩安全人員，假如您穿上長褲、襯衫和外套，我們將非常歡迎您在此用餐。

- order 點菜、點餐、點飲料。

- à la carte 單點。

- young ladies 少女們。

- laugh 嬉笑。

- whisper 低語、交頭接耳。

- croquette 炸肉餅。

- ragoût 法式燴肉。

- chicken croquettes 炸雞肉丸。

- cone 圓錐形。

- leftover 剩菜。

- cheese soufflé 起司舒芙蕾，法式起司和蛋白做的酥餅甜
　　　　　　　　點。

- ham mousse 火腿慕斯，法式甜點的一種，用火腿、奶
　　　　　　　油、雞蛋打成泡沫狀冷凍而成。

- moose 麋鹿，鹿的一種，產於北美，體型大。

- sautéed kidney （法）嫩煎腰子。

- pâté de foie gras （法）鵝肝醬。

- oven 爐子、火爐、烤爐。

- Hors D'oeuver （法）開胃小菜。

- canned 罐頭。

- mushroom 草菇、洋菇。

- au gratin （法）料理方式的一種，用麵包屑和乾酪而燒
　　　　　　成黃褐色的。

- fromage （法）奶酪。

- white sauce　白醬汁，用牛奶、奶油加麵粉調成。
- cracker　餅乾。
- bombe glaceé　（法）甜瓜冰淇淋。
- be serious　正經些。
- naughty　頑皮的、惡作劇。
- bathing trunk　游泳褲。
- bath robe　浴衣。
- barefooted　赤腳。
- pants　（美）長褲、（英）內褲。
- trousers　（英）長褲。
- shirt　襯衫。
- jacket　（美）外套、夾克。
- rule　規則、規定。
- obey order　服從命令。
- properly dressed　穿好衣服的、衣著整齊。
- insist　堅持、不改變。
- very angry　很生氣。
- put on　穿上（衣服）。
- study　學習、研究。
- a pair of pants　一條褲子。
- be pleased to　高興、樂意。
- general manager　總經理。

P. R. director

Mr. Pan, you remember Mr. Winner, the writer for Asia Travel Trade, don't you?

潘先生，你還記得「亞洲旅遊雜誌」的記者溫拿先生嗎？

Mr. Pan/manager

Why, of course. How are you, Mr. Winner? Are you finding enough information about us?

呀！當然記得了，您好嗎？溫拿先生，您對我們的資料搜集完全了嗎？

Mr. Winner

Yes. I've learned a lot. I never realized that the hotel business was so big.

是的，我還學了不少呢！我從來沒想到，旅館的業務還這麼廣。

Mr. Pan/manager

On these occasions it's a pleasant business, too. Everyone likes to eat, especially in nice places. How long are you staying?

在這節慶的日子，這也是愉快的生意，每個人都喜歡在好的餐廳用餐。你還要待多久？

Mr. Winner

I'll be leaving tomorrow evening, I think.

我想，明天傍晚就要離開了。

Mr. Pan/manager

Please come to see me in my office before you go. (A waiter comes up to them with a tray of drinks.)

要走之前請到我辦公室來（服務員端了飲料過來給他們）。

P. R. director

Do you see anything you'd like, or do you want to go to the bar over there?

有您喜歡喝的嗎？或是到那邊的酒廊？

Mr. Winner　This martini looks good to me. Do you want one, too?
這杯馬丁尼（酒）不錯，妳也要來一杯嗎？

P. R. director　(To the waiter) Will you please get me a dry sherry?
（面對服務員）請你給我一杯無味雪莉（酒）好嗎？

Mr. Winner　This is a very colorful room. I like the Mexican decor. May I take a picture of you in front of that mural? No, wait. Let's go over near the buffet tables.
這餐廳的色彩太美了，我喜歡墨西哥的裝飾。妳站在那壁畫前，我給妳拍張照片好嗎？不，等等。我們到那邊靠近自助餐檯拍照好了。

P. R. director　Shall I stand beside the hors d'oeuvres, looking at this pineapple dressed up with cheese cubes, olives, and radishes? Or how about alongside this big fish?
我該站在什錦冷盤的旁邊，看著佈滿起司塊、橄欖和小紅蘿蔔做成的鳳梨。或者靠著這條大魚怎麼樣？

Mr. Winner　No, that fish in aspic is a picture by itself. I'm going to take it in color with a waiter behind the table. I think you'd fit in better with the desserts. Have you ever seen such a beautiful display—all those cakes decorated with fruits and flowers made from colored frosting?
不，這是肉凍做成魚的形狀而已，我要用它和站在桌後的服務員拍彩色照。我想妳站在甜點那裡比較合適，妳看過這麼美麗的陳列嗎？這些所有蛋糕都用水果和彩色的糖花，襯托得這麼美嗎？

P. R. director　We'll have to hurry. Mr. Pan is going to make a speech. Then we may eat. (The waiter offers drinks again.)
我們要快點，潘先生要演講了，我們也得吃點。（服務員又端來了飲料。）

P. R. director　Have another.
再來一點。

Mr. Winner I'll do that. They're good martinis, with just the right amount of vermouth. You may have the olive.
我會的。這是好的馬丁尼，摻了適量的苦艾酒，妳要橄欖吧！

P. R. director Here is the banquet manager. Mr. King, this is Mr. Winner. He's writing about our hotel.
宴會經理來了。金先生，這位是溫拿先生，他來採訪有關我們旅館的資料。

Mr. King It's a pleasure to have you with us today, Mr. Winner.
溫拿先生，我們非常高興，今天有您來光臨。

Mr. Winner The pleasure is mine. This party adds another reason for the success of your hotel. This is one of the most beautiful buffets I've ever seen. I must have a picture of these canapés. What an assortment?
高興的是我。這個宴會使你的旅館，錦上添花，更加成功，我從未見過這麼美的自助餐，我要拍下這些小點心。那是什麼什錦盤？

Mr. King That turkey has been sliced and put together again.
那是火雞肉切片後，再排在一起的。

P. R. director The big three-tiered tray attracts me—jumbo shrimps, lobster, and jellied salmon.
這一大盤排滿了三種東西，真吸引我──大蝦仁、龍蝦、鮭魚凍。

Mr. King In that corner are hot foods. Because this is the Crystal Room. We are serving Mexican dishes today. In the chafing dishes are chicken mole, chili's rellenos and beans, of course.
在那個角落有熱的食物。這是水晶宮餐廳，今天我們供應墨西哥菜，保溫鍋裡有醬汁雞、辣肉丸和豆子。

P. R. director What? No enchiladas or tortillas?
怎麼？沒有肉餅或薄餅嗎？

Mr. Winner That's for me. But I'll need another plate. First I want a picture of the fruit. Will you and Mr. King reach for a mango? (He takes the picture.)
那個給我，我要另外一盤。要拍一張水果照，請妳和金先生伸手拿芒果（他拍照）。

Waiter May I carry your plates? Where are you going to sit?
我來幫您端盤子，您要坐在哪裡？

P. R. director Thanks. Let's sit over there. That table in the corner is ours. I reserved it. (A band of Maria-chis, Mexican musicians, begin to sing and play their guitars.)
謝謝，我們坐在那邊。位子就是我們訂的。
（馬麗亞其斯樂隊開始演奏，墨西哥歌手開始唱歌和彈吉他。）

- writer　作家、記者。

- finding enough　收集足夠。

- public ralation director　公共關係經理。

- ASIA-Travel Trade magazine　亞洲旅遊雜誌。

- so big　很大。

- dress up　裝飾起來。

- realized　想到、真正明白。

- occasion　特別的場合。

- nice place　好的場所、漂亮的地方。

- martini　馬丁尼，雞尾酒的一種。

- dry sherry　雪莉，一種烈性的白葡萄酒，dry在此表示無
　　　　　　味；sweet則表示甜味之意。

- colorful　華麗的、多彩多姿的。

- Mexican decor　墨西哥式的裝飾。

- mural　壁畫。

- olives　橄欖。

- radish(es)　小紅蘿蔔。

- fit in　使適合、調和。

- alongside　靠著。

- aspic　肉凍。

- display　陳列。

- frosting　糖霜，用白糖霜蓋在食品上。

- speech　演講、演說。

- Vermouth　苦艾酒，白葡萄酒的一種。

- banquet manager 宴會經理，主管宴會餐飲服務事宜。
- success 成功。
- canapes （法）用土司麵包切成小塊，加小魚、火腿、牛酪、醬料等，做爲下酒的小菜。
- assortment 什錦。
- turkey 火雞。
- jumbo 大的。
- lobster 龍蝦。
- tier 排滿。
- chicken mole 醬汁雞，墨西哥菜。
- chili's rellenos 辣肉丸，墨西哥菜。
- enchiladas 墨西哥肉餅。
- tortillas 圓薄餅。
- mango 芒果。
- hot food 熱的食物。
- reserved 已經訂位的、保留坐位。
- band 樂隊。

1. 宴會／會議坐位布置方式

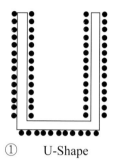

① U-Shape

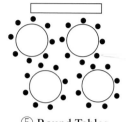

⑤ Round Tables

(dinner/lunch)

(Head Table Optional)

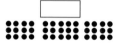

⑥ Theatre Style

⑦ Boardroom Style

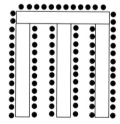

② Hollow Square

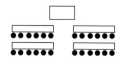

③ Top Table with Sprigs

(dinner/lunch)

④ Schoolroom/Classroom

① U 字型
② 四方中空型
③ E 字型
④ 上課型
⑤ 圓桌型
⑥ 戲院型
⑦ 長桌型

COURTESY: DAWSONS VENUE DIRECTORY, AUSTRALIA

P. R. director

Here we are at the chef's office. Mr. Lee, this is Mr. Winner. He is writing about our hotel, and he'd like to see your kitchen staff at work. Mr. Lee is chief buffet chef. The executive chef isn't here now.

這是廚師的辦公室。李先生，這位是溫拿先生，他要報導關於我們的飯店，他想看看你們廚房工作人員的工作情形。李先生是自助餐的主廚，行政主廚不在。

Mr. Lee/chef

Welcome backstage, Mr. Winner. I'll be happy to take you on a tour. You happened to come at a good time. A wedding reception is being prepared for tonight. Let's begin our tour.

歡迎您到後台來，溫拿先生。我很樂意帶您參觀，您來的正好，有一個結婚宴會將在今晚舉行，他們正在做準備工作，我們就開始參觀吧！

Mr. Winner

Do I have to put on a high white hat and an apron like yours?

我需要像你一樣戴上高高的白帽和圍裙嗎？

Mr. Lee/chef

No, you can't wear our uniform until you can make a baked Alaska or a shish kebab. Over there, as you can see, it's the storage section. Supplies are kept there. These are the refrigerators and next to them is the cold storage room. Would you like to see the centerpieces for the small tables?

不行，假如您會做烘阿拉斯加布丁或串肉塊的話，那麼您就可以穿我們的制服了。那邊您看到的是儲藏室，儲藏備用品。這些是冰箱，隔壁就是冷藏室。您要看看小桌上的擺飾嗎？

P. R. director (Entering the cold room) If I stay in here. I'll look like one of those statues, and I don't feel like Cupid. But they are certainly attractive. Did you mold them by hand?

（進入冷藏室）假如我待在這裡，我會凍得像一座雕像，但不會像是邱比特（羅馬神話中的愛神美童）。這些都很迷人，是用手捏成的嗎？

Mr. Lee/chef Certainly. They're made from butter. Let's go out now. You look frozen yourself.

當然了，用牛油做成的。我們出去吧！您好像凍僵了！

Mr. Winner I've never seen such large pots and pans. Who shines those kettles?

我還未見過這麼大的煮鍋和煎鍋。誰來刷洗這些鍋子、壺？

Mr. Lee/chef They're easily cleaned. The stewards keep this kitchen "spic and span" as you would say. Food doesn't burn or stick easily in these heavy pots. Tableware is washed in electric dishwashers. (He takes the lid off a big pot.)

這些都很容易清洗，管理員把廚房保持得一塵不染。這種厚的鍋子食物不容易燒焦或黏住。刀、叉是用電動洗碗機洗的（他把鍋蓋掀起來）。

P. R. director What a delicious odor! What's that?

什麼味道這麼香！

Mr. Lee/chef It's a special sauce for the casserole. I always have a few warm dishes, even for a cold buffet. We like a variety to satisfy everyone's taste. However, I believe in quality too. Here you can see my helpers preparing the various foods.

Over there the vegetables are washed and peeled.

On that table the meats and fowls are being sliced. And here the salads and cocktails are being made. (He tastes a salad.) This is a very good Waldorf salad, but put in a few more nuts and a little more lemon in the dressing. Jack is preparing avocados here.

那是一種瓦鍋用的特製醬汁。即使是冷盤自助餐，我總會加上幾道熱菜。為了滿足不同人的偏好，我們口味變化多端，同時也很重視品質。您在這兒可以見到我的幾位助手，在預備各種不同的菜色。那邊的蔬菜都是洗過整理好、切好的。那桌上的肉和雞、鴨要切片。這裡正調製著沙拉和開胃菜。（他嚐試一下沙拉）這是很好的華爾道夫沙拉，再放一些豆子和檸檬在配料裡。傑克正在準備酪梨。

P. R. director So that's how avocados are kept green—they're put in lemon water. What will they be stuffed with?

他們把酪梨放入檸檬水中，所以會保持著綠色。那要配些什麼料？

Mr. Lee/chef There's variety of mixtures—fish, minced ham, mushrooms, chicken salad. On that table they are preparing canapes.

這裡有各種的什錦菜：魚、火腿碎肉、草菇、雞肉沙拉等。那桌正在準備小點心。

P. R. director I've never seen so many! There must be a thousand!

我從沒見過這麼多！有一千客吧！

Mr. Lee/chef We'll need about two thousand for the crowd tonight. We try to estimate the exact number so there won't be any waste. Over here is the pastry chef. He's making the centerpieces for the main table.

今晚大概要二千客。我們希望這數字估計準確，以免浪費。那邊是做點心的廚師，他在做主桌用的花飾。

128

P. R. director It's the most original I've ever seen. Look, Mr. Winner. There's a church with the bride and groom standing in front. Is it made from clay?
我沒有見過這樣逼真的。溫拿先生您看，這是一座教堂，新娘、新郎站在前面。是用黏土做的嗎？

Mr. Lee/chef It's made entirely out of sugar. Would you like to look in the pantries? In this one we keep ordinary dishes. In the next one the special chinaware for parties is kept.
全是用糖做的。您要看食品物料室嗎？在這裡我們用來保存一般的盤子，隔壁是存放宴會用的特殊瓷器。

Mr. Winner What are those little baskets on the shelves?
架上的這些小籃子是做什麼用的？

Mr. Lee/chef Those baskets are filled with fruits and sent to important guests.
那些籃子是用來裝水果，送給貴賓的。

Mr. Winner I suppose those buckets are for champagne, aren't they?
我猜那些桶子，是裝香檳酒的，是嗎？

Mr. Lee/chef Yes, and they are also used for room service. The room service department is in this room at the right. Telephone calls are taken here, and the orders are immediately given to the waiters and chefs. Orders are being received now.
是的，也可以用來客房餐飲服務。客房餐飲服務部門，在這裡的右邊。從這裡接受電話點菜，然後立即交給服務員和廚師。現在有人正在點菜。

Mr. Winner (Turning around) This is really a big production. May I take a few pictures? I'd like to show how hard everyone works in the kitchen.

（轉一圈）這真是一個大生產線，我可以拍幾張照片嗎？
我要顯現出每個廚房人員努力工作的情景。

P. R. director How about starting with the stewardess over there?
She's taking out the clean dishes and sorting the silverware in trays. And take one of the cooks who are putting
cakes into the oven over there.
由那位女管理員開始好嗎？她正把洗乾淨的盤子取出來，
和挑揀托盤裡的銀器，然後拍一下那邊的廚師，他正要把
蛋糕放放爐子裡。

Mr. Winner That's a good idea, Mr. Lee. I've certainly enjoyed see-
ing everything here.
這是個好主意，李先生。我很高興能參觀這裡的一切設
備。

chef　廚師

- executive chef　行政主廚。
- backstage　後台。
- wedding　結婚。
- baked Alaska　阿拉斯加布丁，甜點的一種。
- shish kebab　串肉塊。
- supplies　備用品。
- refrigerator　電冰箱。
- cold storage　冷藏室。
- centerpieces　餐桌上的擺飾。
- Cupid　邱比特。
- mold　捏成（造）。
- pot　深底鍋。
- pan　淺底鍋。
- kettle(s)　鍋子、壺。
- spic and span　亮的。
- electric dishwasher　電動洗碗機。
- odor　香味。
- casserole　（法）瓦鍋。
- taste　口味。
- quality　品質。
- helper　助手。
- peel(ed)　去皮。
- Waldorf salad　華爾道夫沙拉，用嫩芹菜、蘋果塊粒調配。
- avocados　酪梨或稱鱷梨，南美洲產的水果。

- lemon water　檸檬水。

- mixtures　多種東西組合。

- estimate　估計。

- waste　浪費；作廢。

- pastry　甜點。

- original　原本的；真的。

- church　教堂。

- bride and groom　新娘和新郎。

- clay　黏土。

- ordinary dish　普通的盤子。

- special chinaware　特製的瓷器。

- shelve　放物品的棚架。

- room service　客房餐飲服務。

- immediately　立刻。

- production　生產、製造。

- to show　給…介紹。

- silverware　銀器。

- sort　挑揀。

- steward　餐具管理員（男）。

- stewardess　餐具管理員（女）。

Mr. Clark　 I'm glad you could come, Mr. Mullen. Let's relax with a drink. What's your favorite on warm day?
我真高興您能來賞光，木連先生。我們喝點酒輕鬆一下，在這暖和的日子裡，您喜歡喝什麼酒？

Mr. Mullen　I think I'll cool off with a tall drink, a Tom Collins.
我想喝杯清涼的飲料，來一杯Tom Collins。

Mr. Clark　That's a good idea. (To the waitress) A Tom Collins for this gentleman. Make mine a Vodka Collins, Mr. Rich, what will you have?
很好，（面對女服務員）這位先生要Tom Collins，給我Vodka Collins，力吉先生，您要什麼？

Mr. Rich　I'll join you for a drink, Mr. Clark, but it will have to be milk. Business hasn't been good lately, and neither have my ulcer.
我會陪你喝一杯的，克拉克先生，不過我想喝的是牛奶。最近生意並不很理想，我的胃潰瘍又犯了。

Mr. Clark　Aren't you feeling O.K. on this trip?
這次的旅行，你感覺還好吧？

Mr. Rich　Oh, yes. As soon as I arrive at this hotel, I always call the public relations director. She has cool milk sent to my room. A pitcher of fresh milk is sent several times a day. You can't complain about the service here, can you?
噢！是的，當我一來到旅館，就打電話給公共關係經理，她送來了冷牛奶到我房裡。每天要送好幾次，整壺新鮮的牛奶，這裡的服務真是沒有話說。

Waitress (To barman) Make another martini. One guy said you put sweet vermouth instead of dry vermouth in his martini. Give me a Tom Collins and a Vodka Collins. I mixed up those drinks and gave two guys the wrong drinks. Also a bourbon on the rocks and three daiquiris.

（面對酒吧服務員）再來一杯馬丁尼，那位說你把甜的苦艾酒代替了澀的苦艾酒，放入他的馬丁尼裡。給我一杯Tom Collins和一杯Vodka Collins。我弄錯了，那二位的酒，同時給我一杯波本威士忌加冰塊和三杯daiquiris。

Barman You'll have to be careful in a crowd like this. But I'm sure that I put dry vermouth in that martini. Did the man drink it all anyway? Perhaps he just wants another. Pass these snacks around. (The waitress passes salted peanuts, pumpkin seeds, smoked oysters and cheese cubes.)

生意這麼好，你要特別小心。我確實是放澀苦艾酒在那杯馬丁尼裡，那個人喝光了沒？或許他只是要再來一杯！把這點心端著走一圈。（女服務員端著鹹花生、黃瓜子、煙燻牡蠣和起司塊。）

Mr. Clark Gentlemen, as president of the Sea-Land Company, I welcome you. Let's all drink to a successful meeting and continued good relations. (The men lift their glasses and drink a toast.)

各位先生，我，海陸公司的董事長，歡迎你們，讓我們為會議成功，以及保持良好關係而乾杯。（他們舉起了杯子互相慶祝。）

Waitress (To Mr. Clark) Sir, if you'd like to order your starters, we'll get them ready for you.

（面對克拉克先生）先生，如果您要點前菜的話，我們已經準備好了。

Mr. Clark

Fine, while we're drinking, you can prepare them. Let's have a look at the menu. When we've finished our cocktails, we'll sit down at the table. Mr. Mullen, the waitress has brought luncheon menus. What would you like for a starter? You have a choice of appetizers or soup.

很好，我們在喝酒，你們去準備菜單給我們看看。我們把酒喝完，再到餐桌。木連先生，女服務員已經把午餐菜單拿來了，您要先來點什麼？開胃小品或湯。

Mr. Mullen

Marinated herring looks good to me.

醋醃鯡魚對我較合適。

Mr. Rich

(To waitress) What kind of sauce does the avocado cocktail have?

（面對女服務員）酪梨開胃菜，你用什麼醬汁？

Waitress

Any kind you wish, sir. It usually comes with a tomato sauce.

先生，隨您的意思，一般用的是蕃茄醬汁。

Mr. Rich

If the sauce has garlic, don't put it on. I'm allergic to garlic. It poisons me.

如果醬汁裡有大蒜，就不要摻，我對大蒜會敏感，會把我毒死。

Waitress

Shall I have the chef fix you an avocado in the shell?

那麼我叫廚師把您的酪梨，放入貝殼裡好嗎？

Mr. Rich

That's good suggestion. You're a clever waiter, young man. Oh, wait. I see fresh corn soup on the menu. Please change my order. I'd rather have a bowl of soup than the avocado.

那是好建議，你很聰明。等一下，菜單上有鮮玉米湯，請更換我點的菜，我寧願喝一碗湯，總比吃酪梨好。

Mr. Clark Waitress, I think we'll have time for another round before we eat.

女服務員，用餐前我們還想再喝一杯。

- luncheon　午餐（宴）。

- cocktail　雞尾酒。

- portale bar　吧檯車。

- relax　輕鬆。

- favorite　喜歡。

- warm day　暖和的日子。

- cool off　消暑。

- tall drink　用長形玻璃杯裝的飲料。

- Tom Collins　雞尾酒的一種，琴酒加檸檬汁加糖水加蘇
　　　　　　　　打水。

- Vodka Collins　雞尾酒的一種，伏特加酒加檸檬汁加糖水
　　　　　　　　冰塊調勻倒入粉內加蘇打水。

- ulcer　潰瘍。

- as soon as　盡快。

- several time　好幾次。

- guy　男人。

- sweet vermouth　甜苦艾酒。

- dry vermouth　不甜苦艾酒。

- mix(ed) up　混合在一起。

- bourbon on the rocks　波本威士忌加冰塊。

- daiquiris　雞尾酒的一種，蘭姆酒加檸檬汁加糖。

- be careful　要小心、注意。

- pumkin seed　黃瓜子。

- smoked oyster　煙燻牡蠣。

- good relation　良好的關係。
- toast　乾杯、舉杯互祝。
- starter　開始，前菜。
- appetizer　開胃小菜。
- marinated herring　醋醃鯡魚。
- what kind of　哪一種的。
- any kind you wish　你喜歡的任何一種。
- tomato sauce　蕃茄醬汁。
- garlic　大蒜。
- put it on　放進去、摻入。
- poison　有毒。
- fresh corn soup　新鮮玉米湯。
- another round　再來一杯。

西餐餐具

品　名	中　文
Dessert Spoon	點心匙
Dessert Fork	點心叉
Dessert Knife	點心刀
Tea Spoon	茶匙
Coffee Spoon	咖啡匙
Fruit Fork	水果叉
Table Spoon	湯匙
Table Fork	餐叉
Table Knife	餐刀
Sugar Ladle	砂糖匙
Ice Cream Spoon	冰淇淋匙
Butter Knife	奶油刀
Butter Spreader	奶油塗刀
Bouillon Spoon	小圓湯匙
Cake Fork	糕點叉
Cake Spoon	糕點匙
Melon Spoon	瓜匙
Strawberry Spoon	草莓匙
Fish Knife	魚刀
Fish Fork	魚叉
Fruit Knife	水果刀
Cream Soup Spoon	濃湯匙
Salad Fork	沙拉叉
Cocktail Fork	雞尾酒叉
Oyster Fork	生蠔叉

Captain (Smiling) Good morning, ladies. Your tables are ready. This way, please.
（微笑著）早安，各位女士，餐桌已準備好了，請走這邊。

Waiter (Helping to seat the guests.) Good morning. Here are the menus. (Waiter fills the glasses with ice water.)
（幫客人入座）早安，菜單在這裡。
（服務員將冰水倒入杯子裡。）

Mrs. Hoffman Oh, you can speak English. How nice for us.
哦！你會說英語，真是太好了。

Waiter A little. We have English classes here at the hotel.
只會一點。我們旅館有開英語課。

Mrs. Hoffman (To waiter) Please take out the ice. I never drink ice water.
（面對服務員）請把冰塊拿掉，我從來不喝冰水的。

Waiter May I take your order, please?
請問，您要點菜了嗎？

Mrs. Hoffman Let's see. We don't have a lot of time. What are you going to order, Lucy?
我想，我們沒有很多時間了，露西，妳要點什麼？

Mrs. Redman I'm not hungry in the morning, but I'm very thirsty. I'd like a large glass of orange juice. Is it fresh, frozen, or canned?
早上我還不很餓，不過我很渴，給我大杯的柳橙汁。那是新鮮的、冰凍的，還是罐頭的？

Waiter It's fresh, madam. We serve only fresh orange juice.

140

是新鮮的，我們都供應新鮮的柳橙汁，夫人。

Mrs. Redman That's fine, and a sweet roll, and coffee. Would you mind bringing me another glass of ice water? By the way, is the water purified?
很好，還要甜麵包、咖啡，麻煩你再給我一杯冰水好嗎？水是乾淨的吧？

Waiter Oh, yes. The water here is safe to drink. (To waiter) Please bring the water pitcher. (To the next lady) What would you like to order, madam?
當然是乾淨的，這裡的水請安心的飲用。（面對服務員）請把水壺拿來。（面對下一位女士）夫人，您要點什麼？

Mrs. Hentz I don't know yet. Bring me a cup of tea first.
我還沒決定，先來一杯紅茶好了。（tea，一般沒有指定，即視為紅茶。）

Waiter With cream or lemon?
加檸檬片或奶油。

Mrs. Hentz With milk, please. May I have it right away? I do miss my early morning cup of tea when I travel.
請給我牛奶，可以立刻送來嗎？我出發遊覽前一定要喝杯茶。

Waiter (To waiter) Please get this lady's cup of tea now, busboy. (To Mrs. Hentz) Do you want anything else?
（面對服務員）請給這位女士一杯紅茶。
（面對漢慈太太）您還要其他東西嗎？

Mrs. Hentz Yes, two soft boiled eggs, three minutes-toast, and marmalade.
是的，二個三分鐘的煮蛋、土司和桔皮醬。

Waiter
Buttered or dry toast?
要不要塗奶油（牛油）？

Mrs. Hentz
Buttered, whole wheat toast.
要塗奶油（牛油），純麥土司。

Waiter
(To the next lady) What would you like to order?
（問下一位女士）您要點什麼？

Mrs. Beemer
I'm not feeling well this morning. I don't want very much—just a little cereal. What kind do you have?
今早我不太舒服，不想吃太多，給我一些穀類的，你有哪幾種？

Waiter
Do you want cooked or dry cereal?
妳要煮的還是要乾的？

Mrs. Beemer
Cooked, I think. It's easier to digest, isn't it?
煮的。比較容易消化，不是嗎？

Waiter
Oatmeal or cream of wheat? How about a nice bowl of cream of wheat with warm milk?
麥糊或奶油麥片？或來一碗奶油麥片加熱牛奶怎麼樣？

Mrs. Beemer
That's fine. Only a small portion, not very much. My stomach isn't very strong.
很好。一些就行，不要太多，我的胃並不太好。

Mrs. Hoffman
Girls, we must hurry. We ought to leave in half an hour. It's 6:30 now.
小姐們，我們在趕時間，半小時之內我們就要出發了，現在已經六點半了。

Waiter
Are you ready to order, madam?
夫人，您準備點菜了嗎？

142

Mrs. Hoffman

This plate of assorted fresh fruits in season—what kinds of fruits are there now?

這盤當令的什錦新鮮水果，現在有哪些水果？

Waiter

Oranges, pineapple, bananas, cantaloupes, figs, strawberries and papaya are in season now.

有柳橙、鳳梨、香蕉、甜瓜（美國產）、無花果、草莓、木瓜，這些都是當令的水果。

Mrs. Hoffman

"Papaya"—what's that?

Papaya（木瓜）是什麼？

Waiter

It's a delicious tropical melon.

這是一種很美味的熱帶瓜果。

Mrs. Hentz

It's very good. We had it in Hawaii last year. It's good for digestion.

很好，去年我們在夏威夷吃過，對消化很有幫助。

Mrs. Hoffman

Bring the fruits, except the pineapple. Don't you have any fresh peaches?

給我水果，但不要鳳梨。有沒有新鮮的桃子？

Waiter

I'm sorry. They're not in season now. We have stewed prunes and applesauce.

對不起，現在沒有桃子（不是產桃子的季節），我們有燉的梅干和蘋果醬汁。

Mrs. Hoffman

No, I prefer fresh fruit, and—let me see—bacon, crisp, and two poached eggs.

不，我要新鮮水果，還有，我想…培根要脆的，和二個水波蛋。

Waiter

Anything to drink?

要喝些什麼嗎？

Mrs. Hoffman American coffee—Oh no, I'll change that to Sanka.
(Waiter leaves to give the orders to the chef.)
美式咖啡，哦！不，給我山卡咖啡。
（服務員把點菜的單子交給廚師。）

Mrs. Hoffman By the way, where is Linda this morning? I don't see her.
對了！琳達在哪兒？今早一直沒有見到她。

Mrs. Hentz She had to cancel the tour. She's not feeling well.
她不舒服，不去遊覽了。

- coffee shop　咖啡廳，供應飲料、簡餐的場所。

- captain　領班。

- to greet (to welcome)　歡迎。

- This way, please.　請走這邊。

- menu　菜單。

- fill　倒入；裝滿。

- ice water　冰水。

- take out　拿走、取出。

- hungry　饑餓。

- thirsty　口渴。

- large glass　大玻璃杯。

- orange juice　柳橙汁。

- fresh　新鮮的。

- frozen　冰涼的、冰凍的。

- canned　罐頭的。

- sweet roll　甜麵包。

- by the way　或者是、順便一提（轉折語氣用語）。

- purified　純淨的、乾淨的。

- drink　喝、飲。

- cream　奶油、乳脂。

- lemon　檸檬、lemon slice檸檬片。

- chef (a cook)　廚師。

- Do you want anything else?　您還需要別的嗎？

- soft boiled eggs—three minutes　三分鐘（半熟）的水煮雞蛋（帶殼）。

- toast 土司。
- marmalade 桔皮醬（塗在土司上食用）。
- buttered or dry toast 土司要塗牛油或不塗牛油。
- wholewheat toast 全麥土司。
- cereal 穀類（穀類加工的食品）。
- cooked or dry cereal 煮的或乾的穀類。
- easier to digest 容易消化。
- oatmeal 麥糊。
- cream of wheat 奶油麥片。
- small portion 少量的、少部份的。
- stomach 胃。
- plate 盤。
- assorted 什錦。
- fresh fruits 新鮮水果。
- in season 當令、盛產季節。
- orange 柳橙（橘子叫tangerine）。
- pineapple 鳳梨。
- banana 香蕉。
- canteloupe 甜瓜。
- figs 無花果。
- strawberry 草莓。
- papaya 木瓜。
- delicious 美味的、好吃的。
- tropical 熱帶的。
- peach(es) 桃子。
- I'm sorry 對不起、很抱歉。

- not in season　非產季、不是出產季節。
- stewed prunes　燉梅干。
- applesauce　蘋果醬。
- bacon　鹹肉條、培根。
- crisp　脆的。
- poached egg(s)　水波蛋（去殼雞蛋，在水中煮的）。
- American coffee　美式咖啡，一般指比較淡的咖啡。
- Sanka (coffee)　山卡咖啡，一種含咖啡因較少的咖啡。
- except　除外、除……之外。

Mr. Hoffman

Whew! That was a longer session than usual. Old Regan surely was going strong, wasn't he? The best idea was yours, Hentz—the coffee break.

喔！這次會議比往常都來得更久。老雷根的確還很強壯，可不是嗎？漢慈，你的主意最好，喝咖啡吧！

Mr. Hentz

No, I don't know. I wasn't listening. But I need more than coffee this morning. I didn't have any breakfast, did you?

不，我不知道，我沒在聽。我只想喝多點咖啡，我還沒吃早餐呢！你呢？

Mr. Foreman

I certainly did. The children woke up about six o'clock. I took them for an early breakfast and sent them off to the zoo. As usual, they are a bigger breakfast then I.

我當然吃了。孩子們六點就起來了，一早我就帶他們去吃早餐，送他們去動物園，他們的早餐吃得比我還多。

Mr. Hentz

When is the next meeting?

下次集會是什麼時候？

Mr. Hoffman

It's a luncheon meeting in the new restaurant. Boss invited a few local businessmen.

是在新餐廳的午餐餐會，老闆邀請了一些在地的生意人。

Mr. Foreman

And a few government officials will also be coming.

還有幾位政府官員也要來。

Waitress

Good morning, gentlemen. What would you like? Do you want a menu?

早安，先生。吃點什麼啊？要菜單嗎？

Mr. Hentz Yes, that's a good idea. But first, what do you suggest for a hangover?
是個好主意。不過,妳對酒氣未消的人,有什麼好的建議嗎?

Waitress Most people order tomato juice with lemon or vinegar, a dash of hot sauce or catsup.
大部份的人叫蕃茄汁加檸檬或醋,少許辣醬或蕃茄醬。

Mr. Hentz That should make me feel better. I couldn't feel worse.
那樣應該會讓我覺得舒服些,不會覺得難過。

Mr. Redman Isn't it after eleven? It's beer time for me. Do you have draft beer?
不是過了十一點了嗎?是我喝啤酒的時間,有生啤酒嗎?

Waitress Yes, we do, sir. We have draft and bottled beer.
有的,先生,我們有生啤酒及瓶裝啤酒。

Mr. Redman Bring me draft, please.
請給我生啤酒。

Mr. Hoffman I'm hungrier than you people. Please bring me an English muffin, toasted, with marmalade, and American coffee.
我比什麼人都餓,給我英式鬆餅烤的,加桔皮醬和美式咖啡。

Mr. Foreman I'll just have a cup of coffee. What happened to you, Hentz?
我來一杯咖啡就好,你怎麼啦,漢慈?

Mr. Hentz　We went to a night club in the hotel, and I drank the local beverage. It's more powerful than the drinks at home. But the show was great. It was better than any I ever saw in the States. (Waitress returns with the men's orders and puts bowls of cheese wafers and potato chips on the table.)
我們到這家旅館的夜總會，我喝本地酒，這裡的酒比我們那兒的更強。節目比我在美國看過的還好看。
（女服務員端著客人點的菜過來，然後放一盆乳酪薄脆餅和馬鈴薯片在桌上。）

Mr. Hentz　Where's my menu? I want to order something else.
菜單呢？我還要點一些。

Waitress　I'm sorry. I'll get it right now.
對不起，我馬上拿來。

Mr. Hoffman　This cup is cracked. I don't like to drink out of a cracked cup. It's not sanitary.
這個杯子破了。我不要用破杯子喝飲料，不衛生。

Waitress　I'm very sorry. I'll get another right away.
對不起，我馬上給您換一個。

Mr. Redman　No, wait a minute. We'd like to go on a sightseeing tour this afternoon. Can you come along to help us?
等一下。我們下午想去遊覽一番，妳可以陪我們去嗎？

Waitress　I'm sorry, sir. I have to work late today.
先生，很抱歉。今天我會工作得比較晚。

150

- session　開會時間。

- luncheon meeting　午餐會談（議）。

- invited　邀請了。

- local　在地的、當地的。

- businessmen　商人、生意人。

- government official　政府官員。

- hangover　宿醉、酒醉未醒。

- tomato juice　蕃茄汁。

- vinegar　醋。

- hot sauce　辣醬。

- catsup　蕃茄醬。

- worse　很糟、很不好。

- draft beer　生啤酒，（美draft）、（英draught）。

- bottled beer　瓶裝啤酒。

- hungry　饑餓。

- English muffin　英式鬆餅。

- local beverage　本地產的飲料，但本文爲「本地產的酒」。

- powerful　強烈。

- States　指美國（U.S.A. = United States of America）。

- cheese wafer　乳酪薄脆餅。

- potato chips　馬鈴薯片。

- on the table　放在桌面上。

- cracked　破了。

- coffee break　喝咖啡休息時間。

Mrs. Hoffman
(To waiter) You work long hours, don't you? You waited on us this morning, didn't you?
（面對服務員）你上班很久了，是不是？今天早上是你為我們服務的，對不對？

Waiter
Yes, madam, I did. But today I'm working a broken shift. I came at six this morning and left at ten. This evening I'm working four hours.
是的，夫人。但我今天上的是兩段班，早上六點來，十點下班，然後今晚再做四個小時。

Mrs. Hoffman
I wouldn't like that shift. I think it would be better to work eight hours straight. We want just a light dinner this evening. We're very tired after a long sightseeing tour. I don't think it's a good idea to eat a heavy meal when you're tired, did you?
我不喜歡這樣的班次。一次上完八小時比較好。我們只要一些簡單的晚餐，長途遊覽把我們累壞了。當你疲勞的時候，就不想多吃了，你說是嗎？

Mrs. White
I'd like to feed the baby first, if you don't mind. I want to feed him myself.
如果你不介意的話，我要先餵孩子。我想親自餵他。

Waiter
Would you like a highchair for him?
您要高腳椅（小孩用的）嗎？

Mrs. White
Yes, please. He'll be more comfortable. Here are three cans of baby food. Will you have these two heated, please? One is lamb and one is green peas.
是的，這樣會更舒適些。這三罐嬰孩食品，其中二罐麻煩你給我熱一下好嗎？一罐是小羊肉，另一罐是綠豆。

152

Waiter Do you want this one heated too?
這罐也要熱嗎？

Mrs. White No that's fruit—apple sauce and apricots. Just open it and put it in a little dish.
那是水果，蘋果醬和杏子，不必熱，只要打開放在一個小盤子裡就可以了。

Mrs. Hoffman Do you always give him canned food?
妳經常給他吃罐頭食品嗎？

Mrs. White No, he has fresh food at home, but these are very convenient for travelling. This is powdered milk. Tell the chef to mix with purified water, please. Does he know how it's done?
不，在家他吃新鮮食品，帶罐頭旅行比較方便。這是牛奶粉，請你吩咐廚師用乾淨的水沖調，他知道怎麼沖泡嗎？

Waiter Yes, he does. I saw him mixing powdered milk for another baby this morning. And he always uses purified water. Don't worry, we'll fix the baby a good dinner.
他會沖的，我早上看過他幫另一位嬰兒泡牛奶，他都用蒸餾水，請放心，我們會給嬰兒料理一頓好晚餐的。

Mrs. White Fine. And would you bring him a toasted crust to chew on? (Waiter goes out and returns with the baby's dinner.)
很好，妳可以給他，一塊麵包皮嚼嗎？（服務員去端來了嬰兒的晚餐。）

Waiter Here you are, Mrs. White, this special heater will keep the bottle warm. And if you out of cans, you can get them here. We always have plenty of baby food.

這裡就是了，懷特太太，這個是特製的電熱器可以使瓶子保溫，如果罐頭食品用完了，這裡還有，我們經常備有許多嬰兒食品的。

Mrs. White
Thank you. I've been sure to bring enough, because I know what he likes. But I can see you know how to look after babies here.
謝謝妳，足夠了，我知道他愛吃什麼，我知道你很會照顧嬰兒的。

Waiter
Would you like to order now?
您現在要點菜嗎？

Mrs. Beemer
I don't have to look over the menu. I already know what I'm going to eat.
我不用看菜單，我已想好要吃什麼了。

Mrs. White
You have to watch your diet, don't you?
妳一定要注意妳的飲食，對嗎？

Mrs. Beemer
Yes, since I've had diabetes I haven't traveled much. But before we came here. We wrote to the hotel and sent them my diet list. I order just what's on my diet, and everything's been fine.
是的，自從我患了糖尿病後，我不敢常常旅行。但是在我們來此之前，已照會飯店，並寄來我的食譜。我只叫我可以吃的東西，所以一直都很好。

Mrs. Hoffman
I watch my diet too, but not for the same reason. Whenever I go on a trip, I gain weight. Then after I return home, I diet. I've already put on five pounds.
我也是在注意飲食，不過理由不同而已，每當我出外旅遊，體重就會增加，回家後再節食。現在我體重已經增加五磅了。

154

Mrs. White (To the baby) Jim, here's a nice crust.
(To waiter) Where's the milk?
（面對嬰兒）吉姆，這土司皮很好。
（面對服務員）牛奶好了沒有？

Waiter Oh. I'm sorry. I forgot it. I'll get it right away.
哦！對不起，我忘了，馬上就來！

Mrs. Beemer Just a minute. You can take my order now, please. I want a small grilled ground sirloin. Don't bring me hamburger. Tell the chef it's for Mrs. Beemer. He knows I must have lean meat.
等一下，我現在要點菜。我要一客小份的烤沙朗牛排，不要給我漢堡牛肉，告訴廚師是畢馬太太的，他知道我一定要用瘦肉。

Waiter Yes, madam. The ground sirloin do you like your steak rare, medium, or well-done?
好的，夫人。您的沙朗牛排要嫩的，半熟，還是全熟的？

Mrs. Beemer I like it medium rare, but not too rare, just pink inside. And bring me string beans, without butter, just plain, and fruit jello.
我喜歡半生熟的，但不要太生，只要裡面粉紅色就好。另外給我豆條，不要奶油，要清的和水果凍。

Waiter And you, madam?
您呢，夫人？

Mrs. Hoffman Cottage cheese and sliced tomatoes, yoghurt, and black coffee for me.
我要軟白起司和蕃茄片、優格，另外給我黑咖啡。

Mrs. White Bring me the grilled sirloin with mashed potatoes.
給我烤沙朗牛排加馬鈴薯泥。

Waiter Do you want mustard or meat sauce?
您要芥末或是醬料？

Mrs. White Mustard, please. And make my steak medium.
芥末。牛排要半熟的（五分熟）。

Mrs. Hoffman Please change my order. I'm going to have the grilled sirloin too, well-done, with scalloped potatoes au gratin. (She sees a pastry nearby.) Don't those French pastries look good! Let's have one of those with our coffee!
我要換菜，也給我烤沙朗牛排，全熟的，和燒烤的干貝洋芋（她看旁邊的糕餅）法國糕餅看來不錯，來一份配咖啡吧！

Mrs. Beemer Don't tempt me! It's not on my diet!
妳不要誘惑我，那東西我可不能吃。

- broken shift　兩段班（早晚班）。

- straight　一直的、不停的。

- very tired　很累了。

- heavy meal　份量很多的餐食。

- highchair　嬰孩用的高腳椅。

- lamb　小羊肉（排）。

- apple sauce　蘋果醬。

- apricot　杏子。

- canned food　罐頭食品。

- convenient　便利。

- toast crust　土司皮。

- chew on　嚼、口中嚼食。

- out of　沒有了、用完了。

- diet　特殊的飲食。

- diabets　糖尿病。

- grilled ground sirloin　烤沙朗牛排。

- hamburger　漢堡。

- lean meat　瘦肉。

- rare　生嫩的。

- medium　半熟（五分熟）。

- well done　全熟。

- medium rare　半生熟（三分熟）。

- Jello　美國一家製造水果凍公司的商標。

- cottage cheese　白起司，以酸奶做的，較軟的乾酪。

- yoghurt　優格、酸奶酪。

- black coffee　黑咖啡，不加糖及牛奶。

- mashed potatoes　馬鈴薯泥。

- mustard　芥末。

- meat sauce　吃牛排時配的醬料。

- scalloped　干貝。

- potatoes au gratin　燒蕃茄。

- French pastries　法式糕餅（甜點）。

- tempt　誘惑。

- put on　增加。

158

Mr. Clark (To waitress) This isn't what I ordered. I want a crab cocktail.
（面對女服務員）這個不是我叫的，我要的是蟹肉盅。

Waitress I'm sorry, sir. I thought you said lobster.
對不起，先生，我以為您說的是龍蝦。

Mr. Rich Look here, waitress. There's hair in my corn soup. Take it away.
女服務員，來一下！玉米湯裡有頭髮，把它拿走！

Waitress Oh, no, sir. Wait a minute. I'll ask the headwaiter if that's a hair.
噢！先生，不會的。請等一下，我問領班怎麼會有頭髮？

Headwaiter (Looking at the "hair") Sir, let me explain. Fresh corn soup is made from corn cut off the cob. That's a piece of brown corn silk, not a hair.
（看那「頭髮」）先生，讓我向您解釋一下，鮮玉米湯是用玉蜀黍穗軸取下的玉蜀黍粒煮的，這是一根黃色的玉蜀黍絲，並不是頭髮。

Mr. Rich Oh, so it is. A piece of corn silk. Well, I'll eat the soup. There's nothing better than fresh corn soup.
哦！原來如此。是一根玉蜀黍絲。那麼，我就喝了。沒有其他東西可以比得上新鮮玉米湯了！

Mr. Clark How about sharing a châteaubriand with béarnaise sauce? What do you say?
叫一份厚牛排配比尼士醬汁合著吃怎麼樣？你說好不好？

Mr. Mullen I usually like a good juicy steak, but today I think I'll have the Dover sole.

通常我喜歡吃多汁的牛排,但今天我想要吃杜瓦的比目魚。(Dover地名,在英國南部。)

Mr. Clark And I'll have roast beef with Yorkshire pudding and a mixed vegetable salad.

我要烤牛肉和約克夏布丁和什錦蔬菜沙拉。(Yorkshire地名,在英格蘭。)

Waitress A mixed vegetable salad with hollandaise sauce? (To Mr. Mullen) The same for you, sir?

什錦蔬菜沙拉加荷蘭醬汁嗎?

(面對木連先生)先生,您也要一樣的嗎?

Mr. Mullen With hollandaise sauce? That has eggs in it, doesn't it? I'm allergic to eggs. They make me sick. Better make mine a chef's salad with oil and vinegar to be on the safe side.

荷蘭醬汁?那不是有加雞蛋嗎?我對雞蛋敏感,它讓我不舒服。給我主廚沙拉加油和醋,這樣比較安全。

Waitress (To Mr. Rich) And you, sir?

(面對力吉先生)您呢?先生!

Mr. Rich I'll have creamed chicken. Tell the chef to give me only white meat—the breast, and the artichoke hearts.

我要奶油雞,告訴廚師我只要白肉 —— 雞胸肉和朝鮮薊心。

Wine waiter Now sir, with your chicken, you'd like a good dry wine— a Chablis, or a Riesling? Perhaps you like a smooth white Burgundy, a Meursault? (Mr. Rich shakes his head.) Would you like a light flowery wine, say, a spicy Pouilly-Fumé or a delicious Vouvray? (Mr. Rich shakes his head.) Then you might like a fruitier wine from late picked grapes, very good with your creamed chicken. (Mr. Rich continues to shake his head.) Well, then, how about a vin rosé? Most people like that.

先生，您要好一點的辛味酒來搭配您的雞肉吧，你要Chablis或是Riesling？也許您喜歡順口的White Burgundy還是Meursault？（力吉先生搖搖頭）您喜歡淡淡的花香酒，有煙燻味的Pouilly Fume，或是美味的Vouvray？（力吉先生搖頭）那麼您也許喜歡果香酒吧！以晚收成的葡萄釀製的，配您的奶油雞非常適合。（力吉先生還是搖搖頭）那麼，玫瑰酒如何？很多人喜歡的！

Mr. Rich They all sound good, and I knew them all from years ago. I've drank them all. But I'm afraid I must drink milk.
這些的確都不錯，幾年前我就知道了，也都喝過了，但我必須要喝牛奶。

Waitress (To Mr. Clark) With your beef, sir, a Chambertin or Cote-d' Or Burgundy?
（面對克拉克先生）先生，來一杯Chambertin或Cote-d' Or Burgundy配您的牛肉如何？

Mr. Clark Chambertin, vintage 1959, if you have it.
Chambertin，1959年份的，如果你有的話。

Waitress (To Mr. Mullen) And you, sir?
（面對木連先生）您呢？先生！

Mr. Mullen How about domestic wines? Would you recommend one?
在地酒好不好？你能推薦嗎？

Waitress Yes, indeed. We have some fine local wines. I like Chablis. It will be fine with your fish.
好的，我們有幾種在地的好酒。我很喜歡Chablis。它非常適合搭配您的魚。

Mr. Mullen I'll try that. I always like to sample local beverages. You'll bring it well-chilled, won't you?
我試試,我老是喜歡品嚐當地的酒,給我冰得涼涼的,可以嗎?

Waitress Yes, sir. I'm sure you will be pleased.
是的,先生!我相信您會喜歡的!

- crab cocktail　蟹肉盅。
- lobster　龍蝦。
- headwaiter　領班、組長。
- cut off　切下、取下。
- cob　玉米穗軸。
- corn silk　玉米絲。
- châteaubriand　烤長條牛柳排，食用時再分切之。
- béarnaise sauce　醬汁的一種。
- sole　比目魚。
- roast beef　烤牛排（肉）。
- make me sick　倒胃口。
- oil and vineger　油和醋。
- creamed chicken　奶油雞。
- white meat　白肉、雞胸肉。
- artichoke heart　朝鮮薊心。
- Chablis　法國產的白葡萄酒。
- Riesling　德國產的白葡萄酒。
- white Burgundy　法國產的白葡萄酒。
- Meursault　法國產的白葡萄酒。
- flowery wine　花香酒（葡萄酒）。
- Ponilly-Fumé　法國產有煙燻味的白葡萄酒。
- vouvray　法國產的白葡萄酒。
- Vin rosé　玫瑰酒。
- fruitier wine　果香酒，如有蘋果、桃子的香味。

- drunk　醉了、醉倒。

- Chambertin　法國布根地紅葡萄酒。

- Cote-d'Or Burgundy　布根地名酒。

- vintaye l959　葡萄豐收年1959。

- domestic wine　國內產製的酒。

- local wine　當地產製的酒。

- well-chilled　冰得正好。

- smooth　順口的、順的。

164

酒杯／酒／餐點

酒杯	酒	餐
apéritifs 開胃酒	SHERRY VERMOUTH CAMPARI	HORS D'OEUVRES　前菜
sparkling wine 汽泡酒	CHAMPAGNE	HORS D'OEUVRES　前菜
white wine 白酒	CHABLIS HOCK RIESLING	FISH　魚肉 CHICKEN　雞肉
rosé wine 玫瑰酒	ROSE D'ANJOU	VEAL　小牛肉 CHICKEN　雞肉
red wine 紅酒	BEAUNE BURGUNDY CHIANTI RIOJA BEAUJOLAIS	BEEF　牛肉 LAMB　羊肉
dessert wine 甜點酒	PORT MADEIRA	DESSERT　甜品
liqueurs 利口酒	LIQUEUR BRANDY COINTREAU	COFFEE　咖啡

COURTESY: FIVE STAR ENGLISH, OXFORD

Mr. Redman

What a day! How about giving us a drink?
什麼日子啊？請我們喝酒怎麼樣？

Mr. Hoffman

I'm going to call room service for set-ups right away. There's half a bottle of scotch and almost a full one of bourbon. Do you want anything else?
我立刻叫客房餐飲服務（以下簡稱客餐服務）來安排，這兒有半瓶的威士忌和將近一瓶的波本威士忌，你還要其他東西嗎？

Mr. Redman

If you don't mind, I'd like a martini.
如果你不介意的話，我要一杯馬丁尼。

Mr. Hentz

Do you have bitters for an old-fashioned?
你有苦汁摻古典雞尾酒嗎？

Mr. Hoffman

I'll order some. (He calls room service) Please send set-ups for three people to suite 1425—glasses, six bottles of soda, two ginger ales, Angostura bitters, a bucket of ice......and, oh yes, a pitcher of martinis...no, not a large one, only enough for about three drinks.
我叫他們送一些上來好了。（他打電話到客餐服務）請安排些東西到1425套房，有三個人，要幾個杯子，六瓶蘇打水、二瓶薑汁水、苦汁、一桶冰塊……和，噢！一壺馬丁尼……不要太大壺，夠三杯就可以了！

Room service

(On telephone) Would you like something else—whiskey, brandy, or...
（電話中）您還要別的嗎？威士忌、白蘭地或…

Mr. Hoffman

No thanks. I think we have enough for now. (The room service soon arrives with set-ups on a cart. He mixes the drinks and hands them to the men.)

不用了，謝謝。我想這樣夠了（很快地客餐服務送來了，安排好在餐車上，他把調好的酒弄好了端給他們）。

Mr. Hentz
Here, waitress. The old-fashioned is mine.
這兒，女服務員。古典雞尾酒是我的。

Mr. Redman
Waitress, are you sure this is a martini? It doesn't taste right to me. It's very weak.
女服務員，這真的是馬丁尼嗎？好像不是我要的，太淡了！

Waitress
Yes, sir. I saw the bartender fix it myself. He uses the best brands of gin and vermouth.
是的，先生，我親眼看他調的，他用最好的琴酒和苦艾酒。

Mr. Hoffman
Let me taste it. (Sipping the drink) Redman, you're crazy. There's nothing wrong with this drink. It's strong. If you don't want it. I'll drink it myself.
讓我嚐嚐看（啜一點酒）力門，你發神經了，這酒一點也沒錯呀！夠濃的，如果你不要給我好了！

Mr. Redman
Give it back, Hoffman.
把它放回去，哈福門。

Mr. Hentz
(To waitress) It won't rain tonight, will it?
（面對女服務員）今晚不會下雨吧，會嗎？

Waitress
It may, sir. It's the beginning of the rainy season.
也許會，先生。現在雨季剛剛開始呢！

Mr. Hentz
Then we'd better stay in the hotel.
那麼我們還是別出去（待在旅館裡）。

Mr. Hoffman
That's all for now, waitress. Here, I'll sign the bill. The service charge is included, isn't it? Let's see. It's ten percent, isn't it? (He hands the waitress a tip.)

通通都有了吧，女服務員，把帳單給我簽名，服務費加上了沒有？我看看，加了百分之十，對嗎？（他給了女服務員小費。）

Waitress

Thank you, sir. If you want anything else, we are at your service.
謝謝您，先生。如果還要其他什麼東西，我們隨時為您服務。

Mr. Hentz

I don't know how you feel, but I'm getting hungry. Some good Italian spaghetti would hit the spot。
我不知道你的感覺如何，我似乎餓了。來一些上選的意大利麵正合我意。

Mr. Hoffman

Yeah, I agree about eating, but I feel like a good steak. (There's a knock at the door. Mr. Hoffman opens it, and another room service waiter wheels in a cart with a big tray of assorted cold cuts, cheese, and rolls.)
是的，我也想吃，不過我喜歡好的牛排（有人敲門，哈福門先生開了，另一個客餐服務員推了一車的什錦冷盤、起司和甜麵包進來）。

Mr. Hoffman

Well! What's this? Is this on the house? Who sent this up?
啊！這是什麼？是旅館招待的嗎？誰叫的？

Waitress

This is suite 1425, isn't? That's the number on the order.
這是1425套房，不是嗎？菜單上寫的是這個號碼。

Mr. Hoffman

Yes, but I didn't order food. Just a minute. I'll call room service. (Talking to room service) There must be some mistake. A waitress has just brought a trayful of cold meats...Yes, this is suite 1425. No, I'm sure that I did not order food. I did order set-ups for three a while ago. That's all. Wait a minute. (To his friends) You guys didn't order this stuff, did you?

168

不過我並沒有叫菜呀！等一下我打電話給客餐服務（和客餐服務講話）可能弄錯了吧！剛剛女服務員送來一大盤的冷盤……是的，這是1425套房。我確實沒有叫吃的東西，我不久前只叫過安排我們三人喝酒而已，等一下（問他的朋友）你們叫這些東西沒有？

Mr. Redman

(Coming out of the bedroom) What? You mean the cold cuts? Yes, I thought we'd like a snack, so I ordered a little something. (He helps himself to a couple of pieces of salami from the tray.)

（從臥室裡出來）什麼？你是說冷盤嗎？我以為我們要吃點心，所以我叫了一些東西（他隨便的從托盤上拿了幾片義大利香腸）。

Mr. Hoffman

A little something! Look at the bill-twenty bucks for cold cuts and cheese!

一些東西？你看帳單——這些冷盤和起司要20元呢！

Mr. Redman

So what? I'll sign the bill. (To waitress) Give me a pen.

是又怎樣？我簽帳就是了（面對女服務員）給我筆。

Waitress

I'm sorry, sir, but the man who occupies the room has to sign the bill!

對不起，先生，應請住在這個房間的客人簽名。

Mr. Hentz

Use your credit card, Redman.

用你的信用卡，力門。

Mr. Redman

Will you accept my credit card?

你接受我的信用卡嗎？

Waitress

Surely, sir. Please sign your name on the bill also. (He compares the signatures. Then he looks at the date on the card.) I'm sorry, sir, but the date has expired. This is February and your card expired in January.

當然可以，先生，請您在帳單上也簽名（他對照簽名，看了卡上的日期）對不起，先生，有效日期已過了，現在是二月，有效期間到一月而已。

Mr. Hoffman

Here, waitress. I'll sign the bill. I didn't know the order was given. Now, can you recommend a good place for dinner, one with a good floor show?

女服務員，我來簽好了。我不知道是我們叫的。我們要吃晚餐，你能介紹一家好的餐廳，並且有好節目的嗎？

Waitress

Have you seen the show in the Crystal Room, our new night club? There's a good show there now with a star from Las Vegas.

我們新的夜總會水晶宮的節目，您欣賞過沒有？由拉斯維加斯來的明星，表演精彩的節目。

Mr. Hentz

Let's go now. I'm hungry, and I want neither cold meat nor cheese.

我們現在走吧！我餓了——我不要冷盤也不要起司。

Mr. Redman

(Pouring another martini) But the cold cuts-they're good!

（再倒一杯馬丁尼）但這冷盤不錯呀！

Mr. Hoffman

Help yourself, Redman. I still feel like a steak. (The two men leave.) And Redman—close the door when you get through.

請便吧，力門。我還是想吃牛排。（二個人離開）還有力門，當你吃完的時候，把門關好。

- room service　客房餐飲服務，把餐點、飲料送到客房的服務。

- old-fashioned　古典雞尾酒，雞尾酒的一種。

- soda water　蘇打水。

- a bucket of ice　一桶冰塊。

- very weak　太淡。

- wheel(s)　輪子。

- some mistake　有些不對（錯誤）。

- stuff　食物／飲料（不同種類的）。

- snack　點心。

- salami　義大利香腸。

- bucks　錢（美語）。

- expired　過期了。

- sign the bill　簽帳單。

- service charge　服務費。

- Italian spaghetti　意大利麵。

- to hit the spot　正好。

- compare　比對。

- brand　品牌。

- cold cuts　冷盤，切片的肉。

- a while ago　不久之前。

- help yourself　自己想要的、自己拿、隨意取用。

- get through　結束。

Mr. Foreman

What do we have here?
這裡有什麼喝的？

Waiter

(Pointing to glasses on his tray) Dubonnet, sparkling cider, and martinis. On that table over there is a very good rum punch.
（指著盤上的杯子）杜本內、汽水和馬丁尼。在那邊的桌子還有非常好的蘭姆雞尾酒。

Mrs. Foreman

I think I'll have the punch. It looks so pretty with strawberries floating on top.
我要混合飲料酒，草莓浮在上面，看起來好美。

Mr. Foreman

No highballs?
有高杯酒嗎？

Waiter

Yes, sir. I'll get you whatever you want.
有的，先生。您要什麼，我們都有。

Mrs. Foreman

Billy, from this assortment of canapés you can find something you like—cheese wafers, pâté, caviar, and...
比利，這些什錦冷盤裡有你喜愛吃的：起司薄餅、酥餅、魚子醬，和……

Mr. Foreman

None of that for me. You know I don't like to eat before a big meal.
那些我都不要，進餐前我不喜歡吃太多東西的。

(The guests chat and drink for a little while until the president suggests that they go into dining area and find their place cards.)
（客人邊聊邊喝了一會兒，主人建議他們進入用餐的地方，找他們的座位。）

Mrs. Foreman　Here are our places, Billy, right in front of the centerpiece. (To waiter, who is helping to seat her) Thank your.

這是我們的座位，比利，在擺飾的右前面。（面對服務員，他幫她入座）謝謝你！

Mr. Foreman　Is that a Christmas tree with all those silver streamers?

聖誕樹全部都以銀色的絲帶裝飾嗎？

Mrs. Foreman　It looks like one, but those streamers are made from crystallized sugar and there are French pastries inside. It's very unusual. What's the matter, Billy?

看上去好像是的，這些絲帶是用結晶的糖做的，裡面還有法國甜點，很稀奇。怎麼啦，比利？

Mr. Foreman　I wish I were more comfortable. You know I never like to wear a tuxedo. Redman over there doesn't have a tux.

我希望我能舒服點，妳知道我很不喜歡穿晚禮服的。力門在那邊，他並沒穿晚禮服。

Mrs. Foreman　Look at the waiters. They're all wearing tuxedo jackets and a bow tie like yours. Our waiter certainly looks well-groomed, doesn't he? That's one thing I've noticed about the waiters and waitresses in this hotel. They always look neat and clean. I like to see waiters with white gloves, don't you? Here comes the soup.

看看服務員，他們也都穿了禮服外套，紅蝴蝶領帶像你一樣。這裡的服務員看起來好像是新郎一般，我注意到一件事，這家旅館的男、女服務員，他（她）們看起來總是整潔、乾淨的。我喜歡服務員戴白手套，妳喜歡嗎？湯來了！

Mr. Foreman
I don't know what this is.
我不知道是什麼湯？

Waiter
It's Vichyssoise, sir.
是青蒜薯蓉，先生。

Mr. Foreman
I think hot soup is better than cold. What else is on the menu? I can't read the fine print without glasses.
我想熱湯會比冷湯好。菜單上還有些什麼？沒戴眼鏡看不清楚。

Waiter
Snails in garlic butter, guinea hen under glass with wild rice, braised endive, heart of palm salad, and croquette.
奶油蒜煮螺肉、珠雞飯、燜菊苣、棕櫚心沙拉和炸肉丸子。

Mrs. Foreman
Oh, good. We can eat the centerpiece!
哦！好了。我們要吃擺飾了。（表示這些東西他都不喜歡吃。）

Mr. Foreman
I'd change it all for steak and potatoes.
我要把那些換成牛排和馬鈴薯。

Mrs. Foreman
Billy, stop complaining. It's a pity you don't like French cuisine, but I see that you're enjoying the wine.
比利，不要發牢騷了。可惜你不喜歡法國菜，不過我看你倒可以享用你的葡萄酒。

Mr. Foreman
I would if I could get a refill. Where's the wine waiter?
如果我能喝的話，我想再喝多點。酒吧服務員在哪裡？

Waiter
I'll get him right away. (At the end of the meal, waiter serves coffee in demitasse cups.)
我馬上叫他。（餐用完後，服務員送上小杯咖啡。）

174

Mr. Foreman
I could never understand why they use these thimbles for coffee.
我不明白他們為什麼用這麼小的杯子裝咖啡。

Waiter
Don't you like the coffee, sir?
您要咖啡嗎，先生？

Mr. Foreman
The coffee is all right, but the cups are too small.
我是要咖啡，不過杯子太小了。

Waiter
I'll keep your cup filled, sir.
您喝完後我會再為您添加的，先生。

Mr. Foreman
No, thanks, but I would like some of that champagne if the waiter ever comes this way.
不用了，謝謝，我想要香檳酒，不過服務員都不到這邊來。

Waiter
I'll get you some, sir.
我拿給您，先生。

(Just as the music begins, there is a crash at the end of the table. The headwaiter hurries over.)
（音樂剛剛開始，桌子的那頭一陣嘩啦嘩啦的聲音，領班很快的跑著過去。）

Headwaiter
What happened?
怎麼啦？

Busboy
A man took two glasses off my tray and unbalanced it. The glasses fell and broke.
有人從我的托盤上拿走二個杯子。失去了平衡，杯子掉下都破了。

Headwaiter
You should never allow anyone to help himself from a tray. Besides, you were carrying that tray on your fingertips. Always carry a heavy tray on the palm of your hand.
你不應該讓人在你托盤上取杯子。況且你用指尖端盤子，你應該用你的手掌來端這麼重的托盤。

(After the entertainment, Mr. Hoffman makes a brief speech and the guests begin to leave.)
（宴會完畢，哈福門先生作了簡短的演說，客人開始陸續的離去。）

Mrs. Foreman
Shouldn't you leave a tip?
你要給些小費吧！

Mr. Foreman
I thought I'd give that fine young waiter a ten-dollar tip, but only two dollars to that lazy wine waiter. (He gives the waiters their tips.)
我想給那個服務很好的年輕服務員十元小費，那個懶惰的酒吧服務員給二元就夠了。（他分給服務員小費。）

Busboy
Thank you, sir. It was a pleasure to serve you. But sir, we usually get twenty-dollar for a banquet.
謝謝您，先生，很高興為您服務。不過，平常每次宴會我們都有20元小費的。

Headwaiter
(Hearing busboy last remark) Busboy, come over here. (Aside to busboy) This will be your last tip in this hotel. Report to the personnel department in the morning.
（聽到見習生以上的言談）見習生，過來這裡（站在見習生旁邊）這是你在本旅館最後一次的小費，明天早上就到人事室報到。（因為向客人多要小費，將被開除。）

- formal banquet　正式的宴會。
- Dubonnet　一種開胃酒。
- sparkling cider　汽水。
- punch　用水果、酒、飲料（果汁）等調成的雞尾酒。
- assortment　什錦的。
- paté　酥餅。
- caviar　魚子醬。
- chat　聊天。
- Christmas tree　聖誕樹。
- streamer　絲帶。
- tuxedo (tux)　晚禮服。
- bow tie　蝴蝶結。
- highball　高杯酒，雞尾酒的一種，威士忌加蘇打。
- neat and clean　整潔乾淨。
- Vichyssoise　（法語）青蒜薯蓉湯（冷湯）。
- snail　蝸牛。
- guinea hen　珠雞。
- heart of palm salad　棕櫚心沙拉。
- croquette　（法語）炸肉丸子。
- French cuisine　法國料理。
- refill　再添加、再裝滿。
- demitasse cup　餐後用的小咖啡杯。
- unbalance　不平衡。
- fingertip　指尖。
- palm of your hand　你的手掌心。
- entertainment　有娛樂活動的宴會。

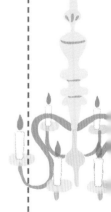

- brief speech　簡短的演講。
- lazy　懶惰。
- personnel department　人事部門。

① 葡萄酒的飲用習慣

1. 使用無色玻璃杯，讓飲用者能確實見到酒的色澤及清澈程度。

2. 將酒瓶出示於你的客人，一瓶好酒足以增加主人的顏面。

3. 西方人習慣喝葡萄酒配菜，用以增加菜色滋味，何種酒配何種菜，並無一定規則，但習慣上，先飲不含甜味的（Dry）白酒，再喝紅酒。還有在習慣上——食用家禽、鳥類、魚貝海鮮、白肉等配飲白酒；食用牛肉、羊肉及乳酪時，搭配紅酒。然而假如你喜歡，在吃漢堡時來杯白酒，或以紅酒來佐中餐，又有何妨。

4. 白酒及玫瑰紅酒在飲用前要予以冰涼，但不能太冰，理想的溫度是攝氏7～10度，太冰了會失去酒的芳香味（Bouquel）。喝飲紅酒是不須冰涼的，一般在室溫下飲用，但在天氣炎熱的地方像台灣與東南亞地區，飲用薄酒萊紅酒時，須稍微冰涼到攝氏12～13度。

5. 開瓶時，先用小刀沿瓶口突出圓圈下方切除鉛封。那樣可以避免酒被落下細碎鉛屑所污染。德國酒通常有一條開封帶，用手將開封帶拉開即可，無須用刀切。

6. 打開軟木塞前後，須用清潔的布巾將瓶口及瓶頸內面加以擦拭乾淨。

7. 有時一瓶陳年佳釀當開瓶後，會在軟木塞邊及瓶內發現少許發亮的結晶體，此等美麗晶體實為瓶中酒最佳保證，因為只有陳年佳釀含有頗多水果成份（Fruit）方能產生此等酒石結晶，斟此種酒時須特別小心，以減少酒石注入杯中。

8. 仔細聞一下瓶塞，因為那樣可以聞到酒的味道，是否純正。

9. 酒杯可以大一些，最好能有六盎司到九盎司容量或更大些，斟酒半滿，則酒可在杯中搖動而使酒香溢出。

10.每開一瓶酒，都須加以試酒。

❷ 牛排的煎法

VERY RARE	很生

只有前表面薄層，肉緣呈紅色，滲出肉血汁，用手指觸壓，肉裡柔軟（soft）。

RARE	生

紅色鮮肉轉為淡紅，肉表層變褐色（茶色），全塊豐滿，上下翻煎壓，貼煎板，使肉血變成肉汁。

MEDIUM RARE	半生熟（三分熟）

肉的內層轉為淡紅色，豐滿狀肉汁呈淡紅，手指觸壓外層稍感堅實，且慢慢變為銀灰色（gry）。

MEDIUM	半熟（五分熟）

肉的內層為淡紅色，肉汁漸少，外表呈褐色（browned），肉緊縮，觸壓時沒有彈性。

MEDIUM WELL	近全熟（八分熟）

淡紅色已消失，肉汁少而淡，看不出紅色，肉質堅實，緊縮（plumpness）。

WELL/WELL DOWN	全熟

整塊肉裡均已呈灰色，肉汁很少，肉質縮小微硬（hard），外層呈乾狀之褐色。

Barman　How are you this evening?
您好嗎？

Mr. Winner　Not so good. I'm afraid I'm catching a cold.
不很好，我想大概是感冒了。

Barman　The weather hasn't been very good. This is a bad time of the year for colds. It's chilly in the morning, hot in the afternoon and windy at night.
天氣不很正常，這是一年裡最容易感冒的時候。早上凍得很，中午又熱起來，而晚上的風很大。

Mr. Winner　Is there a drugstore nearby?
這附近有藥房嗎？

Barman　Yes. There's one about a block and a half away. As you go out the front entrance, turn right. Go across the street and walk east for about half a block. But if you need medicine for a cold, I have something that will help.
有的，離這裡約有一條街左右。如果您從前門走，右轉穿過馬路，向東走半條街就是。如果您要感冒藥的話，我這裡有一些，您不妨試試。

Mr. Winner　What do you recommend?
你有什麼好點子？

Barman　I've cured many colds with a hot toddy of rum and lemon.
我用熱開水調蘭姆酒加檸檬汁，治好了很多人的感冒。

Mr. Winner　O.K. You're the doctor. My father used to say that was good for colds, too. Give me your medicine.

By the way, where's the crowd tonight?

好吧！就當你是醫生吧！我父親也這樣說過。把你的藥給我！今晚什麼地方比較熱鬧？

Barman
It's always quiet on Sunday. People go to the movies or church, or out of town. Here you are.

星期天都比較安靜，人們去看電影或上教堂，有些到郊外。這是您的。

Mr. Winner
Thanks. This is nice and warm. What's that you're stirring now?

謝謝，這個又好又溫暖，摻了什麼呢？

Barman
It's called rum swizzle. I've put in a dash of Angostura bitters so I have to stir. We also put bitter in pink gin to make it pink.

這叫蘭姆雞尾酒，放幾滴苦汁一起攪拌，我們也用粉紅琴酒摻入讓它成為粉紅色。

Mr. Winner
Yes, I know. They use it a lot in the tropics, in soups and sauces for flavoring. They say it comes from the bark of a tree in Venezuela. The recipe is a family secret. Say, whose pretty drink is that?

我知道。在熱帶地方，很多用在湯裡和醬汁裡，增加味道。據說這是由委瑞內拉的一種樹的樹皮得來的，是家庭料理的秘方。噢！那杯美麗的酒是誰的？

Barman
It's for that lady who just came in. It's called a pousse café, made from several liqueurs. Each liqueur has a different weight and one sits on top of the other.

是那位剛進來的女士要的，叫做「普施咖啡」，用好幾種甜酒調成的，每樣甜酒用比重不同，才會一層一層的。

Mr. Winner
It looks like a rainbow. Doctor, you can give me another toddy when you get around to it. Your medicine is helping me. I feel better already. I'm not a connoisseur, but

I'd say this is choice rum. You have a lot of sugar cane in this country, don't you?

好像是一道彩虹。待會兒再給我一杯托迪酒。你的藥真有效，我覺得舒服多了，我雖不是鑑賞家，不過我可以說這是上選的蘭姆酒，你們這兒出產很多甘蔗，是不是？

Barman Yes, and we do have good rum. In your country bourbon is the favorite drink, isn't it?

是呀，所以我們出產上等的蘭姆酒，您那裡出產波本威士忌很出名，對嗎？

Mr. Winner In the South it is. I hadn't drunk it before I went to Kentucky. They say it was first made there. It's distilled from corn, isn't it?

是的在南部，我到肯塔基之前還沒喝過。那裡出產的最早，用玉米蒸餾出來的，對不對？

Barman Yes. All whiskeys are distilled from grains. The Scotch use barley, and the Canadians use rye. Russians use several things for vodka—wheat, rye, corn, and potatoes.

是的，所有的威士忌都是用穀物蒸餾出來的。蘇格蘭威士忌用大麥，加拿大威士忌用裸麥，蘇俄用好幾種東西釀造伏加特——小麥、裸麥、玉蜀黍和馬鈴薯。

Mr. Winner A lot of people are drinking vodka these days. They say it doesn't leave an odor on the breath. I guess it's not so bad as beer for odor. What gives beer its flavor?

現在很多人喝伏加特，他們說氣味很順，我想像啤酒的氣味就不錯了，啤酒是用什麼香料？

Barman Flowers from hops. You've seen hop vines, haven't you?

用蛇麻草的花，您看過蛇麻草蔓嗎？

Mr. Winner Sure. I had seen those before I know about beer. You have to know a lot to be a good bartender, don't you? I've been watching you measuring and mixing, and putting drinks in different kinds of glasses. (Pointing to the glasses on the shelves) Do you use all those glasses—the tall ones, the short ones, the slender ones and wide ones?

看過了。我瞭解啤酒以前就看過了，你要知道得很多，才能當一個好的調酒員，對嗎？我一直注意看你量酒、調酒，然後將酒倒入不同形狀的杯子裡（指著架子上的杯子）你會用這些杯子嗎？——高的、矮的、瘦的、寬的。

Barman Of course. Each drink has its own particular glass. Men had made alcoholic drinks before they knew how to cook. Would you like another?

當然會的。每一種酒都有它專用的杯子。人類在學會燒菜前，就會釀酒了。您要再來一杯嗎？

Mr. Winner No more, thanks. I'm beginning to feel sleepy. I'm going to go to bed. I believe your medicine has cured me. See you tomorrow.

不用了，謝謝！我開始想睡了，我應該上床了，相信你的藥可以治好我的感冒，明天見。

- bar　酒吧、酒廊。

- barstool　酒吧台的椅子。

- catching a cold　感冒了。

- drugstore　藥店、藥房。

- a block　一條街。

- medicine　藥品。

- hot toddy　蘭姆酒加熱水加檸檬汁調配的酒。

- rum　蘭姆酒。

- out of town　離開城市。

- stir　攪拌。

- rum swizzle　蘭姆雞尾酒。

- a dash　幾滴；些微。

- Angostura bitter　產於南美的一種樹皮，提製的苦味液。

- tropic　熱帶。

- flavoring　調味料。

- pousse cafe　餐後酒。

- liqueur　甜酒。

- connoisseur　飲食鑑賞家。

- distilled　蒸餾的。

- Scotch　蘇格蘭威士忌。

- barley　大麥。

- odor (odur)　氣味。

- breath　呼吸。

- Canadian　加拿大威士忌。

- Russian （蘇聯的）伏特加。
- hop vine 蛇麻草蔓。
- particular 特殊的、不同的。
- alcoholic 酒精、含酒成份的。
- rye 裸麥。
- put in 放到裡面、摻入。

酒杯的常識（圖文取材自『餐旅服務 I』五南圖書出版）

Water Glass /
Water Goblet
水杯

Red Wine Glass
紅酒杯

White Wine Glass
白酒杯

Sherry Glass、
Port Glass
雪莉酒杯、
波特酒杯

Brandy Snifter
白蘭地杯

Cocktail Glass
雞尾酒杯

Martini Glass
馬丁尼杯

Sour Glass
酸酒杯

Champagne
Saucer
香檳杯

Champagne
Flute
香檳杯
（鬱金香型）

Liqueur Glass
香甜酒杯

Mr. Hentz

(Tasting his wine) Chambertin is good wine, waitress, but this doesn't taste right. I think it tastes of cork. (To Hoffman)How's yours?

（嚐著他的葡萄酒）Chambertin是好酒。女服務員，不過這瓶好像不很好，我想應該嚐嚐軟木塞才對。（面對哈福門）你的怎麼樣？

Mr. Hoffman

I ordered Margaux. It's the best I've had in a long time.

我叫的是「Margaux」，我一直都是喝這種最好的。

Waitress

(Pouring out a little Chambertin in a glass to sample it) Let me see, sir. Yes, you're right. It does taste of cork. I can't understand it, because I opened a new bottle for you. Perhaps it wasn't stored properly. I'll get another bottle. (He brings another bottle and offers some to Mr. Hentz.)

（倒一些Chambertin在杯子試嚐）讓我嚐嚐看，先生，不錯，要試塞子才對。我不明白，因為我開的是新瓶（未開過的），也許是儲存不適當吧！我開另一瓶給您（他拿另一瓶給漢慈先生嚐）。

Mr. Hentz

Ah! This is perfect. Thank you.

啊！這個好，謝謝你！

Headwaiter

(Coming to their table) Is everything satisfactory, gentlemen? Is the steak to your liking?

（來到他們的桌子）先生，都還滿意嗎？牛排合您的口味嗎？

Mr. Hentz

Yes, they're very good. May I have some more sour cream on my baked potato? And bring some meat sauce, not a hot sauce, just the regular.

是的，很好。再給我一些酸奶油摻馬鈴薯好嗎？並且給我一些肉醬，不是辣醬，普通的就行了。

Headwaiter

I'll have the waitress bring them. May I have the pleasure of making crêpes suzettes for your dessert? I use Grand Marnier and Benedictine in the sauce.
我叫女服務員拿給您。我是否有這榮幸為您調製，「火燒薄餅」甜點呢？我放Grand Marnier和Benedictine在醬汁中。

Mr. Hentz

Personally, I'd rather drink the Grand Marnier straight.
對我自己來說，我寧願喝純的「Grand Marnier」酒。

Mr. Hoffman

While we're watching the floor show, I think we'd rather drink than eat. I'll stay on scotch. Send me a Drambuie.
看表演的時候，喝酒比吃東西要好，我還是喝威士忌。給我一杯Drambuie。

Mr. Hentz

B and B for me.
我要「B and B」（酒名）。

Headwaiter

Brandy and Benedictine, yes sir. I'll give the bar your orders. By the way, gentlemen, the general at the next table thinks that he has met you. He asked me to invite you to join him and his friend for a drink.
Brandy加Benedictine，先生。我叫酒吧送過來。先生，鄰桌的一位將軍曾見過您，他叫我請您跟他們一起喝酒。

Mr. Hoffman

Thank you. Ask the general and his friend if they will be our guests. (The headwaiter brings over the general and his friend, who introduce themselves. They all shake hands.)
謝謝你，我們請將軍和他的朋友好了。（領班把將軍和他的朋友帶過來，他們彼此互相介紹，握手為禮。）

(188)

Mr. Hoffman

General, what would you and your friend like to drink?
將軍，你們喜歡喝什麼酒？

General　Cognac will be fine. (The bar waiter brings a bottle of cognac to the table. Just then lights go off. A spotlight is turned on the stage, which is dark. The curtains, which are black, and a glamorous singer appears. only her white face and golden hair can be seen.)
Cognac好了。（酒吧服務員送來一瓶Cognac，就在這時燈光熄了，聚光燈照向舞台，在布幕暗暗的地方，出現一位迷人的歌手，只能看見她白白的臉和金黃的頭髮。）

General　Marvelous! Bravo! (After the applause, she drops her black coat and steps forward. She is dressed in a tight-fitted sparkling gold dress.)
真是不可思議的！（一陣喝彩之後，她脫去黑外套，走下來。她穿的是很緊、合身的，閃閃發光的金色服裝。）

General　She's the most beautiful singer that I've ever seen. I've been here every night since she arrived. You Americans surely know Miss Anne Murray, don't you? Can't you invite her to our table?
她是我見過的歌手中最美的一位，自從她來這裡，我每晚都來捧她的場。您們美國人一定知道安妮·木蕾小姐的，是嗎？您能請她來坐一下嗎？

Mr. Hoffman　Of course we've heard of her, but we don't know her. She's the one who we saw in Las Vegas, isn't she, Hentz?
我們聽過了，但我們並不認識。她不就是我們在拉斯維加斯的時候看見的嗎，漢慈？

Mr. Hentz　I think so. They all look alike to me.
我想是的，他們看起來都一樣。

General (To the waitress) Waitress, after this song, goes up to the stage and tells Miss Murray that the general commands her to join us at the end of her first show.

（面對女服務員）女服務員，當她唱完這首歌，你到舞台上告訴木蕾小姐，說將軍命令她，第一場演唱完後，來跟我們喝酒。

Waitress (Returning, with a red face.) I'm sorry, general. Miss Murray said that she wasn't in the army, and that she never obeys commands.

（紅著臉回來）對不起，將軍，木蕾小姐說，她不是在當兵，她可以不服從您的命令。

General (Also red in the face) Good for her! I like a woman who shows spirit. Waitress, get her an orchid right now before the first show ends.

（也紅著臉）好妞兒！我喜歡有志氣的女人。女服務員，第一場唱完之前，馬上送她一朵蘭花。

Waitress But, general. It's almost eleven o'clock. All the flower shops are closed! Where Can I get an orchid?

將軍，已經快十一點了，花店都打烊了，哪有蘭花呀？

General That's your problem. Don't you obey orders, either? Find a beautiful fresh orchid and give it to her with my compliments.

那是你的事。你也不服從命令嗎？去找一朵美麗的、新鮮的蘭花給她，說是我向她致意的。

- Nigh elub　夜總會。
- Margaux　法國布根地白酒。
- stored properly　適當的儲藏。
- crêpes suzette　火燒薄餅，法國甜點，用雞蛋調製的薄餅，用時加酒點燒。
- Grand Marnier　法國產的甜酒。
- Benedictine　義大利產的甜酒。
- personally　自己本人。
- Drambuie　法國產的甜酒。
- B and B = Brandy and Benedictine　白蘭地加班尼迪克丁酒。
- to join　參加；一起。
- shake hands　握手。
- Cognac　法國產的白蘭地酒。
- spotlight　聚光燈、投射燈。
- glamorous　美麗動人的。
- marvelous　不可思議的。
- Bravo　（法語）拍手叫好。
- tight　緊身、很緊。
- sparkling　閃閃。
- Las Vegas　拉斯維加斯（美國賭城）。
- look alike　看來好像（一樣）。
- command　指揮、命令。
- spirit　精神、有活力、烈酒。
- orchid　蘭花。
- with my compilments　致意。
- to drink it straight　喝純的、不加任何東西。

Waiter
Good afternoon, sir. What would you like to have this afternoon?
先生，午安，今天您要喝什麼？

Mr. Winner
Nothing right now. I'm waiting for a friend. Here she comes. (To Miss Wang) I was afraid you couldn't make it.
現在不要，我在等一位朋友。她來了。（面對王小姐）我以為妳不能來呢！

P. R. director
I'm sorry I was late, but we had a long meeting. Mr. Pan said he would come soon. Are you all ready to go?
很抱歉，我來晚了，那是因為會議耽擱的關係。潘先生說他馬上就來，您準備回去了嗎？

Mr. Winner
Yes, but I'd like to stay longer. Now I understand why so many people come to this hotel. Besides being comfortable, it has excellent service. Your people are hospitable and courteous. They make guests feel happy to be here.
是啊！我想多住幾天的。現在我已明白為什麼會有這麼多的客人光臨貴旅館，除了舒適之外，同時還有非常良好的服務。你們的從業人員，用心服務又有禮貌，讓旅客感到快樂。

P. R. director
Thank you. I'm glad you feel that way. That's just what our manager had been talking about. What especially has impressed you?
謝謝您，我很高興您有這樣的感覺，這些事情剛剛我們的經理才提起呢！還有什麼讓您印象深刻的嗎？

Mr. Winner
I think the friendly attitude of everyone. When I go into the bar and restaurants, the waiters and waitresses are not only efficient, they are friendly. Of course, the food

192

is good, too, but a restaurant is more than just a place to eat. It's a place where we go to enjoy food and drinks. It's the pleasant atmosphere that makes this hotel popular.

我想還有每個人親切的態度。每當我到酒吧或餐廳的時候，男女服務員他們不但勝任愉快而且親切有禮。食物也不錯，不過餐廳不只是給人吃飯的地方，讓人有享受的感覺更為重要。所以一定要有很爽朗的氣氛，才能使旅館出名。

P. R. director Tell that to Mr. Pan. That's his theme song.

把這個告訴潘先生。這是他的主題曲。（意思是說潘先生是這家旅館的經理。）

Mr. Winner Well, for example, last night. I was alone, so I went into the bar. The bartenders here not only make good drinks but they're good guys. When they're not busy, they talk to us. Last night we had fun. There was a man from Japan, one from America, and one from Sweden. Each ordered the special drink of his country.

舉個例吧！昨晚我很寂寞，到酒吧去了，調酒員不但酒調得好，而且人緣也不錯，當他們有空時，總是和我聊聊。還有一件有趣的事呢！有三位客人進來，一位是日本人，一位是美國人，另外一位是瑞典人，每人叫一杯代表他國家的酒。

P. R. director That's interesting. Could the bartender make what they ordered?

真是有趣。調酒員是否調得出來？

Mr. Winner Oh, sure. He gave the Japanese sake; the American, bourbon; and the Sweden, aquavit.We were an international group.

噢！一點問題也沒有。他給日本人的是「sake」美國

人的是「bourbon」，瑞典人的是「aquavit」，我們像是一個國際團體。

P. R. director

What did you order? Oh, here comes Mr. Pan.
您叫了什麼？哦！潘先生來了！

Mr. Pan/manager

(Shaking hands with Mr. Winner) Since you're leaving this afternoon, we'd like to give you a proper send-off. Here comes the boy with champagne.
（和溫拿先生握手）今天下午您要離開了，我們想給您好好地送行。服務員端來了香檳酒。

Mr. Winner

Thank you. I was just telling Miss Wang how much I had enjoyed your hospitality. (The waiter tries to open the champagne bottle. He takes off the wire and foil. Then he jerks the cork. It pops out with a loud noise.)
謝謝您。我剛才和王小姐說，您對我的招待太親切了。
（服務員試著開香檳酒，他把鐵絲和錫箔取下，然後很快的拉開塞子，發出很響的聲音。）

P. R. director

Oh, dear! The cork hit that man's arm, and the champagne is spilling all over.
噢！我的天啊！塞子打到那位先生的手臂了，酒也全溢出來了。

Guest

(Jumping up) What-what's happening? I've been hit!
（跳起來）怎麼—發生了什麼事啊！我被打到了！

Mr. Pan/manager

I'm very sorry. The waiter was opening a bottle of champagne and used too much force. Does your arm hurt?
很抱歉。服務員開香檳酒用力太大，您的手臂受傷了沒有？

Guest

(Laughing) Well, I'd rather be hit by a champagne cork than a bullet. I've been in a war, and I know!

194

（笑了）原來如此，我情願被香檳酒塞打中，也不願挨子彈，我上過戰場，所以我知道！

Mr. Pan/manager

I'm very sorry. What would you like for the pain? Please order whatever you and your friends would like. Waiter, please take this gentleman's order. (Waiter returns with another bottle of champagne.) (To waiter) Look, waiter. When you open a bottle of champagne, grasp the cork with your thumb and finger, like this. Turn the bottle slowly with your other hand. Try to prevent the cork from popping out and the wine from overflowing. Now pour it slowly. Let's drink to "bon voyage" and a return visit, Mr. Winner.

非常抱歉。您要些什麼？讓我給您賠罪（pain是痛，意即打了他不好意思，而請他喝酒。）您和您的朋友喜歡什麼儘管叫就是了。服務員，給這位先生送酒（服務員又端了一瓶香檳酒）。（面對服務員）注意，服務員，當你開香檳酒時要用姆指和食指抓緊塞子，像這樣。用另一隻手慢慢地轉瓶子，並試著不要讓塞子彈出來溢出太多酒，然後慢慢的倒酒。讓我祝您旅途愉快，並再度光臨本旅館，溫拿先生。

- farewell　送別。

- waiting for　等著。

- excellent service　絕佳的服務。

- hospitable and courteous　週到而又有禮。

- impressed　有印象的。

- friendly attitude　親切的態度。

- efficient　有效的。

- atmosphere　氣氛。

- popular　有名氣、出名。

- fun　有趣。

- Sweden　瑞典。

- sure　真的；沒問題。

- sake　日本清酒。

- proper　正式的、禮貌的。

- send-off (farewell)　送行。

- hospitality　親切的招待。

- wire and foil　鐵絲和錫箔。

- jerk　很快的拉開。

- cork　軟木塞。

- pop out　砰然作響。

- loud noise　響聲。

- spill　溢出來。

- too much force　用力太猛。

- bullet　子彈。

- grasp　抓緊。
- thumb　姆指。
- prevent　提防。
- bon voyage　（法語）一路順風。
- theme song　主題曲。

1. 酒的分類

一、釀造酒：

1. 葡萄酒（WINE）：由葡萄果汁發酵釀造而成，酒精濃度約7%～15%左右。

2. 穀類酒：由各種穀類發酵而成的酒。紹興酒、啤酒等，酒精濃度約4%～25%。

二、混成酒：

香甜酒（LIQUEUR）：由各種果實及添加材料經蒸餾或其他方式製成的酒。酒精濃度約18%～68%。

三、蒸餾酒：

1. 白蘭地（BRANDY）

2. 威士忌（WHISKY）

3. 烈酒（SPIRIT）：

(1) GIN 杜松子酒、琴酒

(2) RUM 蘭姆酒

(3) VODKA 伏特加酒

(4) TEQUILA 特吉拉

(5) AQUAVIT 阿吉維特酒

酒精濃度約40%～68%

2. 葡萄酒味道標示

中　文	英　文	法　文	
辛	BONE DRY	BRUT	（香檳類）
微辛	DRY	SEC	（香檳類）
辛帶甜	MEDIUM DRY	DEMI-SEC	（香檳類）
微甜	SWEET	—	
甜	VERY SWEET	DOUX	

酒齡

V.O.	10～12年
V.S.O.	12～17年
V.S.O.P.	20～25年
V.V.S.O.P.	40年
X.O.	40年以上

啤酒

生啤酒	draught (draft) beer
黑啤酒	stout
淡啤酒	pilsener
濃啤酒	lager

二〇、接待業務

1. The waitress 女服務員 🔊2-2-1

Busboy　Good morning. You're the new waitress, aren't you?
早安。妳是新來的女服務員是嗎？

Waitress　Yes, I am. My name is Mary Fu.
是的，我叫瑪莉，姓傅。

Busboy　Welcome to our coffee shop. I'm Tony Ho, the busboy here. This is my station, too.
歡迎妳到我們的咖啡廳來服務，我姓何，叫湯尼，是這裡的見習生。這是我的工作台。

Waitress　Oh, good. This is my first day, and I'm nervous. Will you please help me?
哦，真好！這是我頭一天上班，有點緊張，請你多多幫忙。

Busboy　Certainly. I'll get the place settings. (He Carries the place setting on a large tray.) Here, Mary, put these place mats on the table. We use these for breakfast and another kind for luncheon and dinner.
當然的。我要佈置餐桌了（他把餐墊放在一個大的托盤裡）。瑪莉，來把這些餐墊放在餐桌上面，我們鋪好給客人用早餐，午餐、晚餐用另外一種。

Waitress　How pretty—green and white.
好漂亮啊！綠色和白色的。

Busboy　The napkins are green and white also. Put them on the left.

餐巾也是綠色和白色的。把它放在左邊。

Waitress They're paper napkins.
這是餐巾紙。

Busboy Yes, but they're large and soft-like cloth. Here's the silverware. (He hands her the knives, forks and spoons.)
是的，這種大的同時像布一樣柔軟，這裡是銀器。（他將刀、叉、湯匙拿給她。）

Waitress Are these real silver?
這些都是純銀的嗎？

Busboy No, they aren't. They're stainless steel. No, waitress, don't put the forks on the right.
不是的，這些是不銹鋼。女服務員，錯了，不要把叉子放在右邊。

Waitress Oh, yes, I know. I put the forks on the left, don't I? Give me the glasses, please. I put them above the knife. Is that right? (She places the sugar bowl, the salt shaker, and the pepper shaker in the center of the table.)
哦，是的，我知道了。我應該把叉子放在左邊的，對嗎？把杯子給我，我把它放在刀子的上方，對不對？（她將糖罐、鹽、胡椒放在桌子的中央。）

Busboy Look, Mary. This glass is dirty. I'll get another one.
瑪莉，妳看看，這個杯子不乾淨，我去換一個。

Waitress (Pointing to another table) There are ash trays on that table, and there's a vase of flowers, too. I'll get some for my tables. (Waitress returns with vases of flowers.)
（指另外一張桌子）在那桌上有煙灰缸及一盆花，我拿一些放在我的餐桌上（女服務員拿了一瓶花回來）。

200

Busboy Oh, look at your uniform! It's dirty!
哦！看看妳的制服，弄髒了！

Waitress Oh, my goodness! The water from the flower vase spilled on my apron! Oh, what will I do?
哦，我的天啊！花瓶的水弄濕了我的圍裙，我該怎麼辦？

Busboy You'll have to change your apron.
妳應該換妳的圍裙。

Captain (To waitress) Waitress, are your tables ready? A group of tourists is coming in early. They're going on a tour, and they'll want quick service.
（叫女服務員）你們的餐桌佈置好了沒有？有一團觀光客就要來了，他們趕著要出發遊覽，所以需要「快速服務」。

Waitress Oh, dear! What will I do? I have to set two more tables!
哦，我該怎麼辦呢？我還有二桌要佈置呢！

Busboy Don't worry. I'll set the tables. Hurry and change your apron. You can't wear a dirty uniform in this coffee shop. And Mary....
不要急，我來幫妳佈置，妳快去換妳的圍裙，妳可不能穿著髒的制服在這個咖啡廳服務，還有瑪莉……。

Waitress What?
什麼？

Busboy Smile, Mary.
要微笑，瑪莉。

- breakfast　早餐，大致分爲：美式或英式早餐（American or English breakfast）及歐陸式早餐（continental breakfast）二種。

- busboy　練習生、見習生、助理服務員。

- station　服務台、工作台。

- coffee shop　餐廳的一種，一般稱爲「咖啡廳」。

- nervous　緊張、不自在。

- certainly　當然可以、好的。

- place setting　擺餐具，把餐具放在桌面上。

- carries (carry)　搬運、攜帶。

- place mat　用餐墊，用紙質或塑膠品，舖在桌上面。

- luncheon　正式的午餐。

- dinner　晚餐。

- napkin　餐巾。

- on the left　放在左邊。

- silverware　銀器、銀質的餐具。

- knive　餐刀。

- fork　餐叉。

- spoon　湯匙。

- real silver　純銀。

- stainless steel　不銹鋼。

- glasses　玻璃杯。

- sugar bowl　糖罐。

- salt shaker　細鹽瓶（罐）。

- pepper shaker　胡椒瓶（罐）。
- dirty　髒的、不清潔。
- vase　花瓶。
- return　回轉。
- uniform　制服。
- my goodness　（驚嘆語）我的天！
- spilled　溢出。
- apron　圍裙。
- group　團體。
- tourist　觀光客。
- tour　遊覽。
- guick service　快速服務。
- smile　微笑。

持托盤tray (roud)的餐廳女服務員

2. The waiter 男服務員 🔊 2-2-2

Headwaiter

Boys, you've seen the schedule on the bulletin board. We're very busy today and we'll all have to be on our toes. You, busboy, will work with three other waiters in the Baron's Table. There's a small luncheon for about twenty men—a la carte service. The rest of you will help here at the inauguration of this new restaurant. There'll be about 500 important people.

各位，你們已經看過公告欄的進度表了，今天我們會很忙，同時，必須要用心做好。見習生你們和另外三位到貴族餐廳，那裡有20人的午宴，點菜服務。其餘的在這新的餐廳準備開幕典禮，將近有500位貴賓要來參加。

Waiter

Sir, can't I work here either please?
領班，我也要留在這裡工作，可以嗎？

Headwaiter

I'm sorry, but we need you in the Baron's Table today. We've already made out the assignments, and each maitre has arranged tables for the new men. In the Baron's Table there will be one waiter for four guests. Here there'll be two regular waiters to each table. You men will help them. The luncheon here will be buffet style, served on long tables on that side of the room. The guests will sit at these fourteen tables on this side.

很抱歉，工作都是事先安排好的，貴族餐廳需要你的幫忙，領班已安排好桌子給新服務員，在那裡一個服務員要照顧四位客人。這裡有兩個服務員就行了，你們協助他們。這裡的午宴是自助餐方式，餐廳的那邊放長桌子。這邊擺14張桌子讓客人就坐。

204

Busboy

The buffet, sir, is it like the cold buffet on the menu?
自助餐，是不是像菜單裡那種涼菜類的自助餐呢？

Headwaiter

No. This is a special buffet, an informal luncheon buffet, where a variety of food will be placed on long tables. The banquet waiters will stand behind the tables and help the guests. At this type of buffet the guests take their plates and choose the food they want. Your men will take the guests to the tables and seat them. If they want anything else, you get it. You also clear the tables. The banquet waiters will pass desserts, and bar waiters will serve wine and champagne. They also serve the drinks as the guests arrive.

不是，這是一種非正式的、特別的，中午的自助餐。在長桌上有各種不同的菜餚。服務員站在桌子的後面，協助客人，這種方式的自助餐，客人拿了盤子，自己選取喜歡的菜餚，然後你們要帶客人到桌子就坐，如果他們選要其他什麼的，你們也要協助，並收拾餐具。服務員會傳遞甜點，酒吧服務員則服務葡萄酒或香檳酒，當客人來的時候也供應餐前酒。

Busboy

Pardon me, sir. What do we put on the tables?
領班，對不起，我們要擺什麼東西在桌上呢？

Headwaiter

Let's set them now. They've already put on the linen—the tablecloth and napkins.
我們現在就來佈置。桌上已舖好檯布和餐巾。

Waiter

These napkins are larger than those in the coffee shop.
這些餐巾比咖啡廳的還要大些。

Headwaiter

Yes, they're dinner napkins. Fold them properly like this. (He demonstrates.) The tableware and flatware for this room are in the sideboard.
是的，這些是晚餐用餐巾，把它摺好，像這樣。（他摺給他們看）餐具和刀叉就在餐具台裡。

Waiter What about the glassware?
玻璃杯用什麼樣子的？

Headwaiter That's in the sideboard also. We'll need water goblets, and both wine and champagne goblets. Put the wine glass on the right of the water glass and the champagne on the right of the wine glass.
也在餐具台裡。用高腳水杯，還有葡萄酒、香檳酒的高腳杯。葡萄酒杯放在水杯的右邊，香檳酒杯放在葡萄酒杯的右邊。

Busboy Here's the silverware. It looks dirty, sir.
這些是銀器。好像不太乾淨，領班。

Headwaiter Yes, it does. Go get a steward. They haven't polished the silver. We won't need soup spoons, fish cocktail forks, or demitasse spoons. Put on the salad forks, luncheon forks, butter knives and luncheon knives, and two teaspoons. Use the crystal salt and pepper shaker. The centerpiece of each table is a red, white, and green floral arrangement in a crystal bowl.
是不乾淨。去叫餐具管理員，他們沒把銀器擦亮，我們不要湯匙、魚盅叉、咖啡匙（demitasse是小咖啡杯，餐後飲用）。把沙拉叉、餐叉、牛油刀、餐刀、茶匙二支放上，用水晶的胡椒瓶、鹽瓶。以紅、白、綠花插在水晶花盆裡，放在每張餐桌的中央。

Waiter Do we put on any dishes now?
現在可以放盤子嗎？

Headwaiter Yes, put on the bread and butter plates. In this room we use the white china with the gold rim. A1so put on bowls for nuts and mints. Busboy, your special job will be to take care of the water goblets. Put a napkin on your left arm to wipe the pitcher. Don't lift the glass when you fill it, and don't make it too full.

可以，把麵包盤、奶油盤放上。在這個餐廳，我們使用鑲金邊的白瓷盤，還要放一個碗裝豆子或薄荷。見習生你負責水杯，拿一條餐巾放在你的左手臂上，用來擦拭水壺，倒水時不要用手拿杯子，也不可倒得太滿。

Waiter (To headwaiter) Do we put the dishes on at the left side of the guest and take them off at the right?
（面對領班）我們上菜是從客人的左邊，然後從右邊收下，對嗎？

Headwaiter That's a good question. Yes, we use the European style here. But always watch the arm of the guest. Never cross a guest's arm. He may raise his hand and hit your dish. How long have you been here?
這是一個好問題。是的，我們是歐洲式的服務，但一定要注意客人的手臂，不可以太靠近客人的手臂。也許他舉起手時，會碰到你的盤子。你來這兒多久了？

Waiter I just came last week, sir.
我上週才來的，領班。

Headwaiter You're a good man. Be alert and learn all you can.
你很不錯，注意儘量多學習。

- headwaiter (Maltre)　（法語）餐廳領班。
- schedule　進度表。
- bulletin board　佈告牌、公告欄。
- on our toes (to be aleft)　親自去做、用心、注意。
- Baron's Table　貴族餐廳，餐廳的名稱。
- a la carte　個別點菜、單點。
- inauguration　開幕典禮。
- important people　貴賓、重要人士。
- buffet style　自助餐式的。
- long table　長形桌，排放自助餐餐具、食品的檯子。
- Informal luncheon buffet　非正式的自助午餐。
- variety　多種的、各種不同的。
- banquet waiter　宴會服務員。
- bar waiter　酒吧服務員（bar maid女性酒吧服務員）。
- wine　酒，通常指葡萄酒。
- champagne　香檳酒。
- tablecloth　鋪在桌上的檯布。
- dinner napkin　晚餐用的餐巾。
- demonstrate　用實物說明。
- tableware　桌面上的物品，如：胡椒鹽瓶。
- flatware　桌面上的餐具，如：刀、又、匙等。
- sideboard　放各種餐具的檯子，通常靠牆邊。
- water goblet　玻璃杯，通常指有腳或高腳的水杯。
- soup spoon　喝湯的湯匙。
- demitasse spoon　小咖啡匙，通常在用餐後，喝咖啡時用的。
- butter knives　奶油刀。

- centerpiece　放在餐桌中央的飾品、擺飾，如花瓶。

- green floral　綠花的。

- butter plates　奶油盤。

- nuts and mints　豆子和薄荷。

- gold rim　金邊，杯盤的金邊。

- to wipe　擦拭。

- pitcher　水壺，有手把的。

- pouring water　倒水。

- European style　歐式服務。

- be alert　要注意、小心。

- steward　餐具管理員。

- white china　白色的瓷器。

- china ware　瓷器餐具。

- to fill　倒入，把水倒入杯子裡。

- to lift　舉起。

- pass the dessert　遞送甜點。

- to put on at the left　由左邊上菜。

- to take off at the right　由右邊收盤。

- one waiter for four geusts　每位服務員要照顧四位客人。

Cashier Are you going to work at the counter with us, Mary?
瑪莉，妳在服務台和我們一起工作嗎？

Waitress Just for an hour. I was working at those tables near the window, but the manager closed that area for a little while.
只是一小時而已。我本來是照顧靠窗的那幾張桌子，經理暫時把它停了。

Cashier This is the place to work. We get the biggest tips here. People are usually in a hurry, and we give quick service. The customers like to speak English to us, too. Here comes a rich-looking gentleman. Why don't you wait on him, please?
這裡是值得工作的地方。可以拿到最多的小費，通常來這裡用餐的客人都在趕時間的。客人也喜歡跟我們說英語，妳看，來了一位好像很有錢的男士，妳過去為他服務吧！

Waitress (Bringing a glass of ice water.) Good morning. What would you like, sir?
（端著一杯冰水）您早，先生，您喜歡什麼？

Guest Can you bring me a lunch menu? It's early for lunch, but I have to go to a meeting.
午餐的菜單給我看看好嗎？這時吃午餐似乎太早了些，不過我要參加會議。

Waitress Wait a minute please. I'll see. (She returns with the menu.) The special for today is beef stroganoff. Oh, there are two other specials—chicken curry with rice and lamb chops with mint sauce.
請等一下。（她拿著菜單過來）今天的午餐是羅宋牛肉，還有咖哩雞飯和羊排加薄荷醬。

210

Guest What's beef stroganoff? Is it good?
羅宋牛肉是什麼？好吃嗎？

Waitress Yes, it's very good. It's like a stew, with cubes of meat in a very good sauce.
是的，非常好吃，用牛肉瑰和上等醬汁燉的。

Guest I'll have that with a half bottle of rosé wine.
就來那道和小瓶的玫瑰酒。

Waitress Do you want soup or salad?
您要湯或沙拉嗎？

Guest The hearts of lettuce salad.
生菜（萵苣）心沙拉。

Waitress What kind of dressing—thousand island, mayonnaise, or French dressing?
要什麼沙拉醬──千島沙拉醬、白沙拉醬（美乃滋）或是法國沙拉醬。

Guest French dressing. And also bring me a shrimp cocktail.
法國沙拉醬。另外給我一客蝦仁盅。

Waitress Would you like to order dessert now or later?
甜點是等會兒或現在要點？

Guest I'll have the French apple pie a la mode, and coffee. (The man eats his lunch hurriedly.)
我要法國蘋果派冰淇淋和咖啡（這位客人吃得很匆忙）。

Guest Please bring me my check. Here, I'll sign it. (He writes the name "Peter Redman".)
請把帳單給我，我要簽名（他寫上「比得‧力門」）。

Waitress Please write your room number, Mr. Redman. (She immediately takes the check to the cashier. The cashier calls the main desk. The man finishes his coffee, leaves a big tip, and walks past the desk.)

力門先生，請寫上您的房號。（她立刻把帳單交給出納員，出納員打電話到大廳櫃檯，那人已喝完咖啡，給了不少小費，從收銀台前走過。）

Cashier Wait a moment, sir. Do you have your room key?

先生，等一下。您有房間的鑰匙嗎？

Guest No. I don't. I left it at the desk. (The cashier dials the main desk and also another number.)

沒有，我交給櫃檯了。（出納員打電話到大廳櫃檯查詢。）

Cashier I'm sorry sir. Your key isn't in the box.

先生，很抱歉。您的鑰匙並不在架子上。

Guest Then I left it in the room.

那可能是留在我的房裡。

Cashier Is this your signature, sir? Do you have any identification—traveler's checks, credit cards, or your passport? (A house detective comes to the desk.)

先生這是您的簽名嗎？您有證件嗎？如：旅行支票、信用卡或是護照等。（旅館的安全人員已經來了。）

Cashier (To house detective) Would you please check this man's room number? He signed his name "Peter Redman", but I know that Mr. Redman just left the restaurant with friends. He signed the bill. This is his signature. (She shows the detective Mr. Redman's signature on the check.)

（面對安全人員）請你查一下這個人的房號好嗎？他簽的名字是「比得‧力門」，但我知道力門先生剛才和他的朋友離開這裡，這是他的簽單。（她把力門先生簽過的帳單

212

給安全人員看。）

Guest But I couldn't have signed it. I was in a meeting.
不可能是我簽的，那時我在開會。

Cashier Mr. Redman came in for a coffee break with some other men.
力門先生和幾位朋友來這裡喝咖啡的。

Guest I won't say anything more.
我沒話可說了。

Detective Yes, you will. You'll tell the police why you forged a signature, and you won't be coming here soon again. Say, I used to see you around other hotels and bars, didn't you?
是的，你應告訴警察，為什麼你要假冒人家的簽名，短期內你不能再來這裡了。嘿，我過去曾在其他旅館和酒吧見過你，對吧？

- counter　工作檯。
- crowded　擁擠的。
- closed　關起來、暫停營業。
- tip(s)　小費。
- customer(s)　客人、顧客。
- special for today　當天（今天）的特餐。
- beef stroganoff　羅宋牛肉，蘇俄名菜。
- chicken curry　咖哩雞肉。
- with rice　附帶白飯。
- lamp chop　羊排（骨）。
- mint sauce　薄荷醬汁，食用羊肉時用的。
- stew　燴、燉。
- heart of lettuce salad　萵苣心生菜沙拉。
- cube of meat　肉塊。
- a half bottle　半瓶、小瓶的。
- rosé wine　法國的玫瑰酒，配食家禽肉、魚肉等。
- soup　湯。
- dressing　醬汁，吃生菜沙拉時調配用的。
- thousand island　千島沙拉醬。
- mayonnaise　白沙拉醬、蛋黃醬。
- shrimp cocktail　蝦仁盅。
- check (bill)　帳單。
- Franch dressing　法國沙拉醬。
- Franch apple pie a la mode　法國蘋果派霜淇淋。

- cashier　收銀員、出納員。
- immediately　立刻、馬上。
- main desk　大櫃檯，旅客住宿時辦理登記的櫃檯。
- room key　客房（房間）鑰匙。
- signature　簽名。
- police　警察。
- forged　假冒。
- identification　身份證明文件。
- traveler's check (cheque)　旅行支票。
- credit card　信用卡。
- house detective　旅館的安全人員。
- little while　暫時的。

Mr. Hoffman We shouldn't have left Redman alone, should we? It really wasn't very nice.
我們不該把力門留在房裡，是嗎？這樣不太好。

Mr. Hentz It wasn't very nice of him to order a tray of food without telling you, either.
他叫了一大盤的東西不告訴你，也是不應該的。

Barman Good evening, gentlemen. What's your pleasure this evening?
晚安，先生，您要些什麼？

Mr. Hoffman I'm going to stay on the same—a scotch highball. (The men order, and the barman serves them their drinks.)
我還是一樣的，一杯scotch highball（酒吧服務員交給他們所點的酒）。

Mr. Hoffman As we came in we saw two men leaving with hotel guards. What happened?
我們進來的時候，看見二個人被警衛帶走，是什麼事啊？

Barman Nothing much. Those men became noisy and were rude to me. They had too much to drink before they came, and they insisted that I serve them. When I refused, they became unhappy.
沒什麼大事。那二人在這裡大吵大鬧，還對我動粗。他們進來的時候就已喝得很醉了，還一定要喝，我不給，他們就不高興。

Mr. Hoffman That's your privilege, isn't it?
那是你的特權，對不對？

Barman It's not only my privilege but it's my duty. We have a good clientele here, and we maintain high standards.

216

I can't have disorderly people ruin our reputation. Besides, those men weren't guests of the hotel. They've been here before, and they'll come back when they're more sober.

這並不是特權，而是我的責任。我們這裡大都是老主顧，我們要維持高水準，我不能讓那些沒有秩序的人，來毀壞我們的名聲。同時這二個人也不住在本旅館。他們來過，當他們清醒時還會再來的。

Mr. Hentz Let's have another one before we go to dinner. When does the floor show begin?

晚餐前我們再來一杯吧，表演節目什麼時候開始？

Barman In about a half hour. You don't want to miss it. The singer is really great. Would you like to order while you are finishing your drinks? I'll send for a waitress.

約半小時後，您不可錯過，是大牌的歌星。您喝完了要不要點菜？我叫女服務員來。

Waitress (Coming from the dining room with menus) Here are the menus, gentlemen.

（帶著菜單從餐廳過來）先生，菜單在這裡。

Mr. Hoffman I don't need a menu. I feel like a steak. I'd like a good broiled T-bone, rare. Do you guarantee it will be tender?

我不需要菜單，我想吃牛排，給我上好的烤T骨牛排，嫩一點，你能保證會很柔嫩嗎？

Waitress Yes, indeed, sir. All our beef is imported from the finest packing house in the world. We also have filet mignons, sirloins, and New York cuts.

是的，先生，我們的牛肉都是最好的進口貨。我們還有烤菲力、沙朗和紐約牛排。

Mr. Hentz
Let's both have T-bones and French fries. Make mine broiled too, well-done. We ought to have our vitamins or something green. Are the fresh vegetables well cleaned?
我們二人都要T骨牛排和炸薯條，我的要烤熟透的。我們應該吃些維他命之類的東西，新鮮的蔬菜洗得夠乾淨嗎？

Waitress
Yes, indeed. They are washed in antiseptic solution. Would you like a fresh green salad with Roquefort dressing?
當然乾淨，我們的蔬菜是用殺菌劑洗過的。您要新鮮沙拉拌羊乳酪配料嗎？

Mr. Hentz
That's fine for me. Do you want the same, Hoffman?
就給我這個好了，你要一樣的嗎，哈福門？

Mr. Hoffman
Yes, I'll look what's coming. (As Mr. Hentz turns, he knocks over his drink.)
好，我要看拿來的是什麼東西？（漢慈先生轉過身時，他弄倒了他的酒。）

Mr. Hentz
(To barman) Oh, darn. Look what I've done!
（面對酒吧服務員）噢！糟糕！你看我做的好事！

Barman
Don't worry. There's plenty more. I'll make you another—on the house. (Mr. Redman, walking unsteadily, comes up to the bar.)
沒有關係，還有很多，我再調一杯給您—免費的。（力門先生搖搖擺擺的走進酒吧。）

Mr. Redman
I thought you'd be up here. You're nice guys to leave me.
我想你一定會上來這裡，好傢伙，讓我一個人留在房裡。

Mr. Hoffman
You were welcome to come along.
歡迎你的加入。

218

Mr. Redman

(To bartender) A double martini, and make it strong. Without ice.

（面對調酒員）給我雙份的馬丁尼，濃一點。不要加冰塊。

Barman

I'm sorry. I didn't hear what you said. Your dinner will be ready soon, gentlemen. The floor show comes on in about fifteen minutes.

對不起，我沒聽清楚您說什麼？您的晚餐馬上好了，先生，十五分鐘內節目就要開始了！

Mr. Redman

Give me a martini! I'm going in to see the show. (As he turns, he falls off the stool.)

給我馬丁尼！我要去看節目（當他轉身時，他跌落到椅子下）。

Barman

I'll get a waiter to help you.

我叫服務員來幫您。

Mr. Hoffman

You'd better call house guards. Redman's a big man. I'll go down with them. He isn't hurt. He's just dizzy.

你還是叫警衛較好。力門是個大塊頭，我和他們一起下去。他沒有受傷，只是頭昏而已。

- bartender　調酒員。
- barman　酒吧服務員。
- hotel guard　飯店的警衛。
- refuse　拒絕、不接受。
- privilege　權利、特權。
- duty　責任、職責。
- maintain high standard　維持高水準。
- disorderly　沒有秩序的、擾亂的。
- ruin　破壞、損害。
- reputation　榮譽、名聲。
- sober　清醒。
- floor show　表演節目。
- miss　錯過。
- broiled　烤的。
- tender　嫩的。
- packing house　食品供應店。
- filet mignon　牛排的一種。
- New York cut　牛排的一種。
- French fries　炸薯條。
- vitamin　維他命。
- antiseptic solution　殺菌劑。
- Roquefort　法國羊乳酪。
- darn (damn)　該死、糟了。
- on the house　招待的，不收費。
- along　單獨、獨自。

- double martini 雙份的馬丁尼雞尾酒。

- without ice 不要加冰塊。

- dizzy 神魂不定、頭昏眼花。

- clientele 餐館之老主顧。

英語／美語用語對照表

BRITISH ENGLISH	中文	AMERICAN ENGLISH
aircraft	飛機	airplane
bill	帳單	check
book-keeper	記帳員	bookkeeper
car hire	租車	car rental
centre	中心	center
chips	炸馬鈴薯片	Freuch fries
city centre	市中心	downtown
coach	公共汽車	bus
colour	顏色	color
engaged	忙著	busy
fill in	填寫	fill out
first floor	二樓	second floor
ground floor	一樓	first floor
grill	燒烤	broil
hall porter	大廳侍者	bell captain
honour	榮譽	honor
lift	電梯	elevator
May to September	五月至九月	May through September

BRITISH ENGLISH	中文	AMERICAN ENGLISH
notes	支票	bills
pavement	人行道	sidewalk
porter	侍者	bellboy, bellman, bell hop
programme	節目	program
pubs	酒館（吧）	saloons
put throngh (telephone coll)	接通（電話）	connect
railway station	鐵路車站	train station
receptionist	接待員	room clerk
return (ticket)	往回（車票）	two way, round trip (ticket)
single (ticket)	單程（車票）	one way (ticket)
taps	水龍頭	faucets
telephone box	電話亭	telephone booth
tin	罐頭	can
traveller's cheques	旅行支票	travelers checks
trunk call	長途電話	long distance call
underdone	生的（烤肉）	rare
wardrobe	衣櫥	closet
wash basin	洗臉盆	washbowl
waste-paper basket	垃圾桶	wastebasket
W.C.	洗手間	toilet

國家圖書館出版品預行編目資料

餐旅英語會話／潘朝達著.
— 初版. — 臺北市：五南, 2016.08
　　面；　公分.
ISBN 978-957-11-8729-7（平裝）

1.英語 2.餐旅業 3.會話

805.188　　　　　　　105013503

1XOU

餐旅英語會話

作　　　者 —	潘朝達
發 行 人 —	楊榮川
總 編 輯 —	王翠華
主　　編 —	朱曉蘋
封面設計 —	陳翰陞
圖片來源 —	IDJ圖庫
出 版 者 —	五南圖書出版股份有限公司
地　　　址：	106台北市大安區和平東路二段339號4樓
電　　　話：	(02)2705-5066　傳　真：(02)2706-6100
網　　　址：	http://www.wunan.com.tw
電子郵件：	wunan@wunan.com.tw
劃撥帳號：	01068953
戶　　　名：	五南圖書出版股份有限公司

法律顧問　林勝安律師事務所　林勝安律師

出版日期　2016年 8 月初版一刷

定　　價　新臺幣400元